Penguin Books
Johnny I hardly knew you

Edna O'Brien was born in the West of Ireland
and now lives in London with her two sons.
She has written *The Country Girls, Girl with
Green Eyes, Girls in Their Married Bliss, August
is a Wicked Month, Casualties of Peace, The
Love Object, A Pagan Place, Zee and Co.,
Night, A Scandalous Woman and Other Stories*
and *Mother Ireland*, her first non-fiction
book.

Edna O'Brien

Johnny I hardly knew you

Penguin Books

Penguin Books Ltd, Harmondsworth,
Middlesex, England
Penguin Books, 625 Madison Avenue,
New York, New York 10022, U.S.A.
Penguin Books Australia Ltd, Ringwood,
Victoria, Australia
Penguin Books Canada Ltd, 2801 John Street,
Markham, Ontario, Canada L3R 1B4
Penguin Books (N.Z.) Ltd, 182–190 Wairau Road,
Auckland 10, New Zealand

First published by Weidenfeld and Nicolson 1977

Published in Penguin Books 1978

Copyright © Edna O'Brien, 1977

Made and printed in Great Britain by
Richard Clay (The Chaucer Press) Ltd
Bungay, Suffolk
Set in Monotype Baskerville

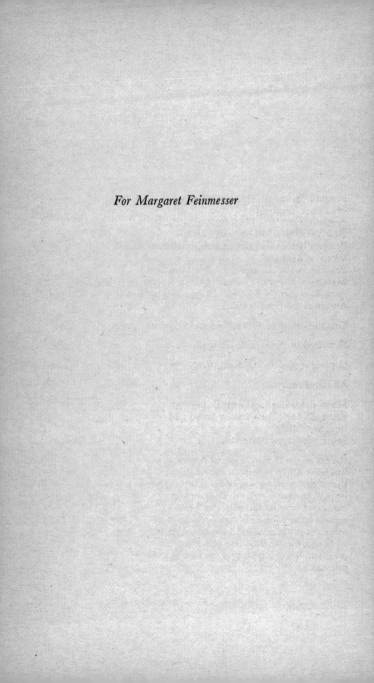

For Margaret Feinmesser

A mother is only brought unlimited satisfaction by her relation to a son; that is altogether the most perfect, the most free from ambivalence of all human relationships.

SIGMUND FREUD

For when our passions
Such giddy and uncertain changes breed
So we are never well, till
We are mad indeed.

Tomorrow I shall have to tell them. I shall have to stand
in that court and tell them why I did it. But how can I
tell them when I do not know why. How can I say we
were happy as sandbirds, and also to stress my happiness
would stand me in no good stead, and oh merciful God,
I like life now that I am in the gravest danger of losing it.
So I will try to tell them as best I can and perhaps ask
them to fathom it, to piece it together. Do murderers do
that?

I'm new at this role although I've been in a court
before, for the custody of my child; but that was long ago
and yet I remember exactly how the sockets of my teeth
wobbled. I knew the judge favoured me; you can tell by
a look but of course I was younger, winsomer, then. The
wear and tear had not shown although perhaps it had
begun to burgeon and was waiting for some supremely
wrong moment to show itself to say, 'Here I am, your

blemish, your scar for life.' It's like that with the face and with the body and even with the hands that grope out mindlessly for any bit of communion on any street corner, for lumps of human bait. Nevertheless, tomorrow, I will pay particular attention to how I look. Before the night is through I will put curlers in to make quiffs, and do *A*'s and *E*'s to make the face muscles taut. In the end good looks are the chief weapon of a woman although they may lead her down into desperate straits, into the gutter. Yet if she keeps those looks through thick and thin she is the winner, she is above them all, at least to outside appearances, and believe me most people go by appearances. I learnt that from Dame Dora who mowed men down with her glacial beauty. Maybe blame Dora, that would be a gas; to cite women such as her who do succeed because they are too cunning to be wholehearted and too wary to go down into the depths where men dread to go. Like slippers or champagne glasses. Dame Dora assured me that she too hollered and bit her own kerchief but I have no evidence of it and I think she told me a pretty story to win my favours. I never really gave her a place in my heart, never ever. Maybe I was grudging but chiefly she did not measure up to my standards, she did not melt, although she used the word about a man I liked and whom I even liked enough to have slide into my dreams and become one and the same person as my own mother, and lift me carefully out, like a sheaf, through an opened plate-glass window. To rescue me it would seem. Aren't dreams a bit of a lark. I liked him, this man of Dame Dora's, and yet he did not know successfully how to kiss me. He put too much energy, too much expertise and effort into it, whereas I like the effortless, at least when it comes to the hunches within the body. This boy and I achieved that. I shall call him Hart. The very first day he kissed me I knew. His lips were like a stream, a stream straight from the hills. After he'd kissed me he bent down, shy, because my son was there and they were colleagues.

'I'll dream about that,' Hart said, and I betook myself out of my kitchen and up to bed for an afternoon sleep so as I could think about him and mull it over. I smelt sex – that vague wandering unerring particular smell. It was on my pillowslip or else it was imaginary, or else it was a warning or it could have been from the previous man. Ah the previous man. No better than the others and probably no worse. He was called Dee and when I first saw him not a flicker of attraction gurgled through me, so much so, that I commented on his tie in order to give him some little gratification; then instantly I forgot his name. But he won me over. How did he win me over? He was kind. He put an arm around me and asked if my shoes hurt. They were lovely suede shoes, jet black, sleek as young kittens, and with the suede unblemished. Above them ankles and legs, thin and thoroughbred as he said, and above that the black hemline of my dirndl skirt, the skirt itself a blazing red silk, and underneath the flames starting up. The flames that we are so afraid of by day, and grapple with by night. We say to ourselves: 'Where will it all lead us to?' and coax the fates to take us on to disaster.

'My head in your lap,' Dee said and I could picture it, his blond head of hair, his soft uncertain face, his teeth in my crotch, outside the skirt, and then a little spate of time or no spate of time, and then his lifting the skirt up and getting his tongue sweetly inside the edging of my lovely or unlovely gusset and reinstating the

9

sweetness, the moistures of other times. It had been a long time since anyone nested there. Sometimes for frail relief the slow rhythmic strokes of the hairbrush and the fancying of some thrashing, thrusting buccaneer. Then there were those damnable walks that I took every afternoon to look at shops, to kill time, to think of my son who was poised to leave; lingering in cafeterias, anything to postpone the beasts of loneliness. Nights chock-a-block with emptiness. Then suddenly Dee pulling the knickers down, the suspenders still affixed to the charcoal-coloured stockings, and the nice lackadaisical way I lay back on my sofa, and lifted my legs right up so that the soles of my feet were facing the cracks on the newly papered ceiling, and shame was banished as I asked for more and more sucks, and just gave into it utterly, as his tongue wound round and round, and I was pleasured in both channels, and in my mind able to bask in the wantonness of it without apologising and thinking of him. Haven't I always been attending to a him, and dancing attendance upon a him, and being slave to a him and being trampled on by a him?

Oh lamb of God who watches over the lilies in the field, why did you not stop me when I was doing it – not the little harmless venial, sinning, suckle but the crime that has led me here. It all began the day Hart kissed me then hung his head saying in a mutter that he would dream about it. I went up to my bed and smelt the other man, or smelt a memory or smelt in future anticipation and I smiled and thought, 'I will be seeing Hart, he is after all my son's best friend.' I thought how nicely it would occupy and freshen a summer, and then I went off into a little side-road of sleep and all I can say is that it was disturbed sleep because I wakened and found I had been shouting, and my cheeks were puffed out as if my mouth had been full of cursing and swearing. I thought, 'My dear, why are you full of vexation when the sun is beaming, the flowers in your garden are bright and upstanding, and the summer has yielded Hart and he will not harm you, he will not prostrate you like all the others.' So why the curses. Why cheeks puffed out with rage. Is it Dee, I asked. Because of course there is a snag, a positive discord to the Dee story. Did anyone think it could be that nice, that pleasant, that rewarding, what with suckles and the faithful guarantee: 'You wait, I will make you happy.' Promises of visits at all hours, of lovemaking at all hours, and in different frames of mind and body, promises of holidays, promises of dawns, of being nudged awake with as light a stroke as a feather and upon being told those promises the mind itself leapt to the possibility of white and grey doves' feathers massaging and soothing its old rag-bag of thoughts. Promises. Are they not the worst, are they not the real villains of affection. One thinks on them, one goes over them searching and accumulating. Like jewels in a box, that one lifts the lid off in order to look in. They shine. Even in the dark. Then most of all, this ruby or that emerald or that snowy pearl. Dee had to make himself scarce. He had a wife and children waiting. I know that story, that unpretty story, those waiting wives, those creatures to whom guardian angels give the first inkling of infidelity, long before a little love letter is found or a phone call is overheard or an intimate present is recognised as something that the husband did not buy in the souvenir shop for himself. Dee came a few times but his hackles were up. It was like he had left the confidential part of himself in the boot of his car. He had not left it at home, he had not left it under a silver salver, he had brought it so far, but no further. Around that time he crashed his car, probably to remind himself that evil spirits were darting about. Then he sent flowers and used for signature the name of a song we both liked. It is called 'Carrickfergus'. It is the usual beguiling upsetting Celtic song with loneliness at the core – loneliness and loss.

> The sea is deep but I can't swim over
> Neither have I wings enough to fly . . .

As I opened the crinkled faces of the pale pink peony roses that Dee had sent, I damped them with a sponge and all of a sudden I saw his face, his affections and all those lavish promises dissolve before me, and I knew that he could not honour what he had said. His wife was worsening. She had collapsed twice in the heatwave, while washing blankets. Collapse was not uncommon that sizzling fortnight in London because the heat had in it the frenziedness of death. It was heat that lay like a glaze over each and every person, and all substances seem to wilt and burn under it. Some liked it, basked in it, jumped into streams and rivers, undressed in public places, whereas some, like Dee's wife, washed blankets and expired. God only knows why she washed blankets unless martyrdom was sister to her and being married to him perhaps it was. Always busy, busy with his camera, going click-click as he took photographs all the time. Having to go abroad too to photograph wars, or famine, having to capture human nature in all its glory, all its pity and all its shambles. People like him even make grief interesting but that is because we have lost our true sights. He shows us the worst but makes it fascinating. He perpetuates lies. But who am I to cast aspersions?

We will come to my crime, and the madness of it, but what preceded it was much madder. Certainly I should have killed long ago. It was mere blunder and restraint that stopped me. Killed the mad father with the long gaitered shins, or the mad mother whose insides I visualised as a bowl of surping and usurping blood. Maybe I should have killed Dee, do his collapsing wife a service. He is not innocent in this, by no means. He would telephone me to say that he would telephone me on the morrow. He would make a point of saying that he had been up all night, and I was meekly to infer from that that he was not making love to his lawful wife, a woman I believe who had plaits, and I will never see her unless they come to court. He might come to try and take photographs of me. My God, I can hardly credit it, that I will have to stand up in the dock, that I will have to answer questions, be cross-examined, that I might even break down and that then one day after weeks and weeks of it I will know my sentence. All I see, foresee is my own self backing away from it with the force of an animal and they will have to hold me down. There is something terrible about a given sentence of time, something irreversible, although our lives are that. And what will my son say as he sits there hearing all and wanting perhaps at times to intervene, to contradict, to say 'My mother is not a harlot' or whatever. Blood is thicker than water but blood nor water carry no issue in a time like this. I even wonder how many members of the public will come, and for what reason and I also wonder if in the dock I should need a glass of water will I be able to ask for it. I dread that I might sweat, there is nothing so unbecoming as sweat on the upper lip. I will be under lights, scrutiny. How much unvoiced censure will there be?

My son brings me gifts. Once a book on games of Patience and another time a box of crystallised violets. Flowers are not permitted here so he placed a few rose petals inside a letter. They were soft and creamy and reminded me of gardens; the big gardens of country houses where I often walked along paths with five or six men taking off their caps to me; hollyhocks and dahlias, bushes with flowers or berries, borders dividing up the walks. Then, as if I were carted there I imagined a drenched garden, everything wet from a recent fall of rain, the light a wonderful phosphorescent yellow, and the little birds beside themselves with glee because of the rain and because of the big wet worms in the aftermath. I once stood in such a garden and not too long ago. Dee and I were there, lolling against a trunk of fallen tree after he had photographed me and oh yes, undoubtedly I was beautiful. Beauty was everywhere. Six or seven red deer bounded out of a thicket, swept past us and then pirouetted away up a path to where there was a beautiful moss-covered nude statue of a boy. You would think we had willed them and asked them to appear for us, asked for their little shy dance, asked for their departure. 'Magic,' Dee said. It was true for that afternoon, for those hours, or is it more exact to call them minutes, to say 'We left the hotel at three, we finished taking the photos at half-past four, by then it was five.' It was not there we embraced but it was there it became planted in us and maybe after that we both conspired to kill it without our knowing. The embrace, not that it means a jot now, was on a long stretch of beach with the tide out and the water distantly lapping. I had sat on that beach during the day when the tide was in and I had watched with utter mesmerisation the in-and-out flapping of a great collar of seaweed that had adhered to a bottom step. It was infinitely monotonous and one would have expected the seaweed to tear itself away from the step, to do anything rather than adhere to the savage certainty of a tide that blew it inwards and then ribboned it outwards. It just obeyed. I would watch it and then watch the lighthouse and each time be surprised by its lovely pale silver twinkle and then I would look at the stray dogs, the mongrels, as they sniffed at one another, or cocked a hind leg, or mounted one another for a little cursory unity while in the back of my mind I was thinking how Dee could give me a nice dinner that night and buy select wines and insist that I eat and even squeeze my hand under the table. His hand, his right hand, was covered in eczema. I can see it now and I can pity it. It looked so raw. I bear Dee no grudge. He merely acted like all of us – mindlessly, thoughtlessly. That in fact would be my defence were I allowed or were I advised to conduct my own case. 'Ladies and Gentlemen, I acted mindlessly and thoughtlessly.' My handsome lawyer would not approve. He is a tall, dark, capable, upright, man and he does not want to know whether or not I did the crime, why I did the crime, or what I feel about the crime and its intricacies. He wants us to wriggle through it, he wants me free.

My son says that he is keeping the house tidy, makes a point of telling me how he hoovered or put cardinal red polish on the tiles outside the front door. Probably remembers the way I used to nag about tidiness and complain that I ran a laundry for him, that I shouted at him once. I raved like an animal. All over a phone call. Over the price of a phone call. His girl friend Judy had reversed the charges and I did not approve of that because I liked human consideration. There will be sniggers if I use that phrase in court. I have just remembered something, something terrible – Hart's parents will be there and at any moment they can look at me or scowl or just pierce me with a glance. It is them I dread seeing. Parents, two people who must have doted on him. I doted on him. He was a beautiful boy. Maybe they have slides or moving pictures of him, him in knickerbockers, him in sailor suit, him on prize-giving day, with his miraculous smile. I wonder if they ever shouted at him, if like me, his mother flew into a rage and said 'get out of my house', and regretted it a second later.

It was when I heard that he had gone to Paris that I felt in me the first gust of warning. Paris, I thought? To whom? With whom? Why? He and I had made some tentative plan to go to a theatre, a puppet theatre no less. At once I searched out a suitable postcard and sent it to his house with an enquiry. I did not put love, or regards at the bottom. Everything about it was reserved, almost curt. Yet the postcard itself had a funereal touch. It was black and depicted an elderly man in a black carriage driving down a leafy road. One felt that he was driving to a funeral. Maybe even his own funeral. I wonder how many mourners Hart had at his. I expect there were a lot of young people weeping and gnashing away. His graveyard adjoins his old school. He wanted to be there. My son will not say whether or not he attended, or subsequently got in touch with the family, whether he sent wreaths or condolence; he will not disclose a word on the matter. He is deathly pale. I suppose something has hit him. The enormity of it all. He is growing a beard too. I do not dare ask him why. I know why. I said to him on the last visit – 'I did love Hart', and he looked down at his boots. They were only laced halfway, as the laces were too short.

Suddenly he said he had wonderful news. It concerned a walk, a little excursion that they had made. He, his girl friend Gila, another boy, and a Dalmatian dog. They had come upon a very old uninhabited cottage and he had managed to wedge the window open and haul out a letter that was one hundred years old. It thrilled him. I saw that that was what I lacked. Awe. What did a hundred-year-old letter signify? He then said that the dog loved muddy streams and we both laughed. Oh to be loved by him. Incest raising its little tonsured head. It must be the nearest thing to birth, to couple with one's own, to reunite. It may sound bizarre but I did love Hart. Except that love has so many twists and turns to it and is by no means the tender shoot it is reputed to be.

Since I came in here and have stacks of leisure my fancy runs away with me and I liken love to a great house, a mansion, that once you go in, the big door shuts behind you and you have no idea, no premonition where it will all lead to. Chambers, vaults, confounded mazes, ladders, scaffolding, into darkness, out of darkness – anything. Sometimes you get left there all alone, stranded, while the loved one has got out, has bolted and gone away and what do you do then; you sit or you cry or you scream or become insensible. What do you do then. I loved like that once. Even the bloody statuary spoke and crumbled. I loved like that once. It was before Hart. The pre-figuration you might say. I shall never forget his stoop, his dun tweed jacket, a spill of straight dark brown hair, and how to denote amusement he would tap one nostril lightly with his forefinger as if he was trying to drum music into himself. I thought Dee might drum him out, drive the last spectre of him out. People do efface each other. He was called Jude. Our little ruses were infinite. I made Carageen Moss for his ulcer. I donned top hat and cane for him. I wore a kimono for him. I had only to see his underpants billowing upon the clothes line, take them and put them beneath me to feel the most enormous surges of pleasure. Pleasure that was then substantiated when I told him so as he hurried to the room or to the pantry or to the garden or wherever, to serve me. At times we were shy. We were so shy that the chewing of toast was a source of embarrassment to us both. We had of course our sorrows. The baggage from our former lives.

One day stands out, beyond all others, for its bleakness. It was during an occasion when he was vowing to leave his wife, but not leaving. They were in the city together; she staying in one house and he more or less in mine. He had left his shaving kit and his suitcase in her abode which meant he had to go there for it but each of the three times he went she was out. She was shopping he thought. On the fourth day he went and the maid was there. His wife was still shopping. He collected his suitcase. I was upstairs when he came in, on my knees praying, if you please, praying that all would be well. He came into the bedroom and kissed me where I knelt. Then he put the case on the bed and said 'Don't be surprised if there are ladies' shoes in here', then he snapped the latches open. There were two pairs of ladies' walking shoes, identical, except that one pair had a bit of brass chain above the toecap. They were black. Then he picked out a little fur animal that must have been for his son. All of a sudden and without its being wound up it played a tune and I tell you that tune smote both of us. It was such a wan little voice pertaining to be animal, though God knows what animal, and to me anyhow it was the very same as if his son was pleading.

'He always wanted one of these,' Jude said with a remarkable restraint. Then he closed the lid of the case and we held on to one another and I remembered a moment when I had first met him and he had told me of a lithograph he and his wife possessed, a valuable lithograph, and it depicted two storm-tossed people, a man and a woman, and I knew that our hour was up but foolishly I tried to defy time. It was arctic in that room and we both had goose flesh. We were going to live in the country but without any salutary warning he went back to his wife and cultivated prize potatoes.

Don't ask me what happens between people. They will ask me in court, they will maraud me with questions. They might as well ask me why daisies are the way they are. Jude's daughter once made a prize daisy chain, several yards long, and he rang to tell me so. It was a

Sunday morning. His wife, Sibyl, had left. He was arriving within a few days, but drinking the last of the cellar wines, bidding goodbye to a shell of a house. He rang to tell me about the daisy chain and I had a very pleasant mental picture of a lawn, and early morning, moisture, father and daughter out there spending what seemed like their last Sunday morning together. It did not come true. I think we know not what we do. Some think they do know and make such a to-do about it and intone important gibberish such as 'The matter will have to be attended to', or 'I do not like the sound of it', but all they are making is noises, farts, in between their sluggish digestings. Do not think that I am saying there is no cheer in this world because there is! There are veritable saints, creatures as meek as lambs, beautiful gardens, parks, chairs and tables to dine off, shops that surpass each other in sheer fairy-tale luxury, bone teacups, tureens, bridal outfits, veils, rivers, harbours, ships, annual outings during which people laugh and picnic and come home late at night and flop on to their beds, to rollick. There are the seashores with their intimations of eternity.

This place is getting me barmy. In a matter of weeks I suffer all kinds of fluctuations – the gamut as it is called. I even feel that everything will be favourable. In such moments I exclaim, I say – I understand all, I forgive all, I see all, I can even face the future with equanimity and then it's gone, and 'Who's Dina', or 'I hate you', or 'Help' volleys out of my mouth.

I cannot say that at the beginning I chased Hart. The opposite. He asked if in the neighbourhood could he telephone. My son was going away, with, as it happened, the wrong girl. He had not exorcised the previous girl and we will come to that, that ache. It seems Hart was not in the neighbourhood but a week later he had the terrible conviction that I was alone and being seized by it. Without that hunch, without that brotherly thought, it might never have come to fruition. But he did call and we took a stroll in the public garden. The grass was yellow and nondescript and all the blades had lain down in dejection, being parched. Not being used to walking together, we kept bumping into one another. My limbs were like half-set jelly. I thought he looked older than his years.

'Have you always been old?' I asked.

'Always,' he said as if it were some kind of joke. Later we went to a cafe and had tea and a buckwheat pancake. It's like a school photo so far away does it seem. That night he stayed. My son and he looked at picture books while I prepared the dinner. As I recall it they ate considerable amounts and with relish.

'Is it all right to stay?' he asked. He knew it was. A young girl, a hussy, called to offer me some limes and seeing him she let out a wow and then lingered. She was full of gabble about her weekend in the country, and all the limes. He smelt them. Then we had to make a drink, to use twists of them. In no length she was tipsy and offering him a bed for the night. Out of deference he hesitated, looked at me, looked at her, and wondered if he was in everyone's way. Very smartly I got up and moved like a demonstrator in a shop, to boast of my sofa. I removed the velvet-covered cushions and then with a sort of nonchalant pull of the lever demonstrated how in a jiff it converted into a double bed. He slept in it.

I had not removed the plastic covering around the mattress and in the morning the poor boy was in a lather. I felt for his feet under the eiderdown saying that I wanted to massage them. Then I put my hand under the eiderdown and then I saw him blush – his feet were moist, in fact they were sweating. I stopped massaging them. But I suppose he realised how he was being seduced.

It has rained since I came here and my son tells me that the grass is growing. It seems that the grass is sprouting up, green, all over the place and the parks are back to normal. Such is the power of longing that after he told me so I dreamt of high blue-green prairie grass, each blade with a bright sheen, frogs and insects and baby birds darting through the undergrowth. I dreamt it here. My son featured in it. He was lying down with his straw hat over his face, wearing his khaki suit. It was the very same as if Van Gogh had painted him. Van Gogh knew a thing or two, but think what it did to his brain, banjaxed it.

Yes, decidedly it is autumn. Shafts of sunlight come through the high-barred window and bathe the room. Of course I want to be out. I like autumn. I get it all mixed up in my head, so that it is not so much a season as a suffusion of beautiful colours. It used to be my lucky season. It was then I visited Sweden for the first time and beheld all the little birch leaves, like millions of sovereigns dancing in the woods, outside Stockholm. How they fed the eye. I was unattached at the time. I had begun to feel numb in the genitals and thought that perhaps attachment, courtship, consummation and all that were too trying and too arduous. The only other person about was a woman and her dog. A strange woman. She had gone into herself. You can tell by the appearance, by the clothes, the walk and a sort of smile. At once I did not want to be like her. I decided that I must have a lover and for a change that I would have a woman. Ah foreign travel! All it needs is a bit of luck, leisure, dalliance, a significant look, and one is in clover. I found one. She was a woman whom I had corresponded with, because she owned a gallery.

Propriety itself marked the early stages of our meeting. We visited a new museum and she cried, so moved was she by the pictures. They were just circular points, black and blue-black points on huge scapes of milky canvas. The museum was all glass and the woods outside and the leafy branches were randomly reflected on the surface of the pictures. I could not understand why she cried being as she was such a haughty woman, a finicky woman. Then we walked in the grounds and she told me about her family. She was half-German and had grown up on the east coast of Africa where her father had a coffee plantation. She missed the wild. She sometimes would lean down to look at a mushroom or a toadstool but she never picked one. Finicky. In her house we sat sedately on high-backed leather chairs and had tea and cinnamon toast. It was her own little salon and the walls almost bayed so covered were they with skins and heads. I heard a footstep. Her husband, she said, had come in and was probably going to rest.

We had a sauna before dinner and it was there as she undressed, in the gloaming, as she smeared oil over her exquisite body that I came up behind her and put my arms around her and made such a fuss of her, and did such coaxing that soon, she was telling me how to rub the salt into her body, how to press it into the crevices. The only light was from the luminous switch on a gigantic machine. There was a smell of pine as she bent and ladled liquid on to the coals. I did not leave go of her and soon she was shivering and aiding my fingers and expressing such exceptional delight. Her quim was as warm as jam that had just been lifted off a stove. Quite a little damson she was and tart to the taste. I played havoc with her hair and knew that she would have to wear a turban at dinner. What would her husband say? Perhaps he approved. I made her straddle at one point and tell me exactly what was going on and she liked that, she liked being queried and was saucy about her little transports and the thoughts behind them. Then I asked her to swing from the top bar of the bunk and so she did, she swung like a puppet. I realised that I treated her like an object, like a sort of bronzed doll, with fur around her neck. Her odours were at once sweet and fetid. Afterwards she said 'Do you think we will get to know one another,' and like any male philanderer I found myself wriggling out of it, voicing an excuse, inventing an appointment.

She sent me a photo of herself the following Christmas, a photo in which she is peering out of furs, like a beaver out of its hiding. There was a very charming message on the back. She meant nothing to me. I must have been far away from myself at the time.

That is another thing, I have left my house, with all my belongings, my secrets and my letters for anyone to pillage, all those letters like cries from the ether. My mother's letters the most pitiful of all. One I have in my purse and I suppose I shall always have it now. It was written after I had sent her a photo. It says:

'I should have written you two days ago when I got your photograph which was very beautiful. It is really lovely and I shall treasure it whatever length I live. I am glad you keep well despite drawbacks and I am glad that you are busy. We are well here and life is as usual only the day I got your photograph didn't the postman kill one of our little lovely dogs, one of our Wicklow dogs so you see we are not lucky with them. The poor little fellow lived in agony for ten or eleven hours. The vet wasn't available to do anything for him but when he did come he could do nothing. We are in bad luck with them but thank God it is only the dogs. We must not complain. You promised to let me know what the little gift for Christmas can be. Do not refuse me as it wouldn't be Christmas at all if I didn't send some little thing. In the spring you will come to see us. I'm looking forward a lot to it – that's fine but then there is the going away. Isn't life full of sadness. My undying love to you.'

I delay all decisions as to what to do with them, as to whether they should be burnt or put in bundles with ribbons round them; until I know what they will do with me. The power of God is hardly comparable with their powers once one is caught. It is the finality of it that buggers me. My lawyer says that there is no use becoming morbid, to keep one's spirit up. I asked him if he thought women hope more fulsomely than men but he did not reply. I think they do, I think their wombs seem to gush hope despite severe jolts and kicking. I think he thought I was bonkers. I consider myself sane compared with my neighbours, my former neighbours strictly speaking. There was a charming woman with massive hair and a double-barrelled name. She found tadpoles in her morning milk and telephoned as many people as one decently can in such an emergency. First she rang her parents who were holidaying abroad, then her doctor, then the milk factory, then a public health officer, and then an artist friend. Not that she got a reply from each one but she made the gestures, that is the thing, to make the gestures. She was advised by one or other of these sources to rinse her mouth with TCP and to rinse her children's mouth with TCP. People do seem to court catastrophe and are constantly referring to disaster or near disaster, about the baby cracking its skull on a Napoleon chamber or the car crashing into a lamp post, or their thyroids capable of producing pellets big as crab apples, usually in the groin. These offerings were announced in the highest of voices, in the highest of spirits. I used to meet the people in the garden in the mornings when I went for a little constitutional. They would be walking their dogs or wheeling their children and I would be striding out with the aid of my malacca cane. It was in case I got the staggers and to ward off vicious animals.

Sometimes I went there at night when it was private. I even regarded it as my own. Jude asked me to carry out a tray of Irish Coffee for his friends. It seems they could hear the glasses rattling before they actually sighted me, and in anticipation they clapped. It was midsummer, but moonless, and the red roses were like beautiful dark blots on the stapled bushes, the pigeons rustled among the trees and our love as I thought was inextinguishable. He must have thought it too, because long after I was in my own house and picking up a silver locket, an heirloom, I opened it and found to my astonishment a scrap of paper folded up to the size of a finger-nail. It was from Jude to me. For a second I thought he had crept back in there and left it but no, it had been written ages before, a year to be precise. It was on the billhead of a restaurant. It said, 'Candles, your round eyes, and my inextinguishable love.' Oh God what masquerading goes on in this world. If I were free now I would tear it up. It is redolent of all that is dead and gone.

It was before they got me that was worst. For ten days I foxed them. I would repeat the rigmarole to myself, the one I had repeated to his colleagues how we were together, how he felt a fit coming on and how I went to the chemist's to get the right medicines. How I came back and gave them to him. How he fell asleep. How I crept out so as not to disturb him. How he must have died in his sleep. They believed me. I then hoofed off to another part of Scotland, said my work took me there, to a castle. My work was to restore pictures. Galling. To think that I could bring a cheek back to life, give it its due of paint or turpentine, rub life-likeness into it, make it seem to breathe again, to think that I could take a ravelled sleeve and make it whole again, the very same as if I'd stitched it, and not only that, but the canvas itself might be falling apart, riddled with holes and I could take it and piece it together. I find it bizarre. As he died the colour in his cheeks came and went like dye.

SO THE CASTLE was a stronghold where I could hide. It was built of stone, a pretty stone of soft pink, and a horse-shoe stairs led the way to the studded oak door. As I stepped into the entrance hall I felt that I had stepped into immunity. No one could dare follow me there, not even his ghost, since castles have their own ghosts, their own watchers. I was told 'Her Grace' was waiting in the Morning Room and passing through the inner hall, just scanning the ancestral portraits and the great dazzle of sword metal, I felt that I was resuming my former life. Work and etiquette would rescue me. Yet a peculiar thing happened. The handle of my teacup came away on my finger. I had not wrenched it, not wrested it. It simply adhered to me and I wore it like a ring, while my hostess first flinched and then most graciously laughed. We put it into a denture box so as to send it to the china menders and then she suggested that I take a rest. Perhaps she sensed my unease.

My bedroom was a bower. It faced the woods. Autumn, this self-same autumn was just beginning and so the pines and the spruces seemed more proudly green as the rest of the wood was a blur of red and bronze, that by degrees, as I pre-imagined, would become more of a red and more of a bronze until the whole landscape was drenched in those colours. There was a donkey outside. The very epitome of unedifying melancholy. It brayed. The lady-in-waiting warned me that the owls would snore at night. They might even scream I thought. Did anyone guess that I had come almost immediately from a deathbed. Outside a swarm of birds were preparing to leave. It was an amazement the way they wheeled and darted about, the way they assembled and scattered again as if they were testing their powers, their convening, and their might. The lady-in-waiting said they were heading for Africa. She had unpacked for me. I said that would be all. She did the brasses while inside I paced the room and tried doing little doodles to see if I would get away with it. Everything was an omen, for good or bad, the birds, their convening, the miserable donkey, the overhanging rocks and boulders that guarded the woodland path. I must walk there, I must risk being struck by a boulder. Suddenly I dragged on a trench coat and hurried out even though I knew the lady-in-waiting had run my bath.

In the woods, helped somewhat by the air, the drip of trees, and the peacefulness I resolved to ring the chemist's. Once I had rung the chemist everything would be better.

During dinner I got a bit pompous. I talked about the drapes, the furnishings, the different designs in fabrics; I talked about the pictures throughout the house and said how I was looking forward to my work to restoring their old lady, their Rembrandt, with the brown gnarled hands. I even told them about my previous job, about how I'd gone to Tuscany to restore a picture for a millionaire and how I had never seen him, I had only heard his peacocks cry. They said how amusing, what fun. The only thing that jolted me was any sudden sound. Any little thud or bell made me jump like a yo-yo. I thought that if I got through a month they would not find me.

Then I would remember where after years, even decades, how a particular murder was traced, and then whatever room I was in and its contents would swim and clatter before my eyes, and my heart would spring as if trying to get up my windpipe and out of my mouth. After dinner I rang the chemist and said that I'd given their name by mistake for getting tablets. They seemed to attach no importance to what I said. Then I rang my son and he said the remains had been sent down. I told him about the pictures, the duck we'd had for dinner, the size of my bath towel, all sorts of gibberish. I think he thought that I was distracted out of grief. It might have rested there but for that one mistake in ringing the chemist's. I believe it is a common lapse. I have heard of a criminal – not one in my class – just a petty thief, who checked into a country hotel and quickly incurred the suspicion of the manager by ordering exotic drinks, highballs and things. He was a labouring man and the madness of his taste brought suspicion to his bedroom door. You could say I brought it on myself.

At times I am fair and I do admit that I must pay for this death. At other times I rage and hit this wall and say I have been paying for crimes all my life, ones that I did not commit, the sins of my fathers, etcetera. Then again I say that to kill him – loving him as I did – constituted the truest and most perfect of sacrifices. They'll reach for their Bibles for that. The right side of my hand is grazed from hitting the wall. I hit with it most forcefully. For hours I am left to my own devices, because of not yet being condemned. One of the warders even asked me if I'd ever used henna, asked my advice. She had mousy hair. The other is a monster. She hears me muttering and before I know it there is a boot in my arse. I had flopped on to the floor the other day to do a bit of praying and invocation when in she came with a yard-brush and as much as swept me up. I think she's jealous. Vicious. She thinks, 'A woman canoodles with a young boy, then kills him and then tries to get away with it!' I acknowledge having been a monster at times, the way I wanted to kill my own father, the way I gloated over it. I hacksawed him bit by bit, then decided on a bit of incineration and having tucked him into the big grey boiler I let him burn slowly, then opened a little slide door and when the pieces were well charred, picked them out on fine brass tongs, for display. Then I consigned him to the most forgotten, most secluded, most scalding and most ignominious corner of hell. They will say Oedipus. Oedipus my arse. What about God? God. In idler circumstances when no one was looking, I tugged when I could not separate two clothes hangers, could not procure the garment I was looking for.

He loved my clothes. Hart did. Had no disapproval of them and no disapproval of me either. He did confide how once in his early teens he took exception to his mother's need for beverages. Coffee upon wakening, a whole flask of it; then more coffee at eleven, a sherry at noon, afternoon tea and a gin promptly at six. But I was able to point out to him his little irrational irritation about that and he just laughed and said 'Yeh'. They lived somewhat formally; he lived on one floor and his parents lived on another, they had an intercom. I expect they were weaning one another away except that it does not happen like that. I reason aloud with myself that he would have died anyhow, that he was on the short list the way we all are. I bore him not one scrap of malice. I had begun to love him. He was just unlucky. That will be a funny thing to say. If the judge asks me to explain myself and if I am able to articulate, I will wander through the whole pit of life and say he was the culprit, or she was the culprit, they all were. I may even go to the marriage bed. I will not start in the marriage bed. It is too solemn. Maybe cite that half bottle of champagne, ordered by my husband, for four at the frugal wedding breakfast. I will make them laugh, tell how my wedding night was interrupted because stones were hurled through the window as the righteous male members of my family arrived in a posse to strike the lovers apart. It is true I was under age. I might describe how my husband lifted the rifle from above the stone fireplace and fired three shots sending the stunned party in a blasphemous scuffle, on to the daffodil avenue. It was a night in spring. Sweet lovers love the spring. Before shooting at them he tried to reason with them, in his stand-offish way. Soon they attacked, kicked him in his most vulnerable place, grazed his jaw and removed a few precious ribs from his thinning brown hair. They said they would brain him. Then as he took action and as the smell of gunpowder filled and clouded the room they were scuttling off, and suddenly driving away in pandemonium. I was hardly able to look at him. His diatribe had commenced, blaming me for them, combining me with them. I kept saying sorry, sorry, and our roles were cast. What I remember is the boiling and re-boiling of a kettle of water on the primus stove, to steam his wounds.

There was an old servant who looked after him and she took a dislike to me. She used to sit or rather stoop on the hob of the range, and say that she had a presentiment that the former Mrs, the raven-haired beauty was coming back, to take up residence. She used to describe the former Mrs who had a horse, and how she used to go riding each morning and meet other people, meet gentry up on the moors. 'I'll read your cup,' she'd say, grasping it from me and then she would go 'ha ha' or 'ho ho' or 'he he' as the tidings in my cup boded ominous.

The days were long. I would go out on the mountain, very often dressed in the former wife's clothing. At least I wore her raincoat, and her wellington boots. There was nothing to do, not even berries to pick. I would go Baa-Baa to the mountain sheep who were too dense or too inept to run away. Then I would hop from boulder to boulder and muse fancifully on Miss Lucy Grey who lived on a wide moor and who had no comrade or no mate. I stayed out there all day to fill time. My husband waited in the big dark gaunt sitting-room, doing something exacting, such as his accounts or taking one of the clocks to pieces. At times he would talk, at times he would glare, at times he would say 'Come here', and I was the happy receiver of a paternal kiss or a paternal pet.

I can hardly think of the marriage bed, my mind shudders, or rather slinks away. In some instances it bears a resemblance to the murder of Hart in so far as I cannot believe that I was present while it was happening. Though it happened, I have the greatest difficulty in recalling what took place. There was of course the big bare-boarded bedroom, the four-poster bed, a small persian rug, a tilley lamp that leaked, odds and ends from the previous wife such as a powder bowl and knitted slippers; outside there was the lonely moorland to remind one of one's romantic incarceration, and everywhere the trees offering an uncommon amount of groaning even on windless nights. But the feelings themselves have vanished or else they were never there. It is so hard to decide afterwards, to know what went on, particularly as no word or no movement lingers on in the mind as being potent with love or happiness. Yet the words and movement did take place and a child was conceived and its birth was to replace the birth of a previous child by a previous marriage. So for two people it was a question of an event carried out and endured for reasons that existed long before it and were not relevant to it. I do not know my own reason – perhaps it was for punishment.

I was afraid of my little child at first, afraid of its rawness, afraid its screams would rupture the rush plaiting of its cot, and when I hold him to me now I wonder if those first uncertain weeks have not made him a little unsteady in this universe.

As a little lad he remembers how I dressed in the mornings, out on the landing, both for modesty's sake and so as not to disturb my husband who slept until noon. In those days I sported a corset. My son says he loved the metal eye of each corset as it was being hooked and loved when all the hooks were closed and I drew on my white slip, then frock then cardigan and then it seems I would go in and embrace him not realising that he had been spying upon me and we would go down and sit at the high service table together and partake of breakfast. I often gave him sweets then, because officially he was not allowed them. Once at a point-to-point two garrulous ladies gave him glacier mints which he accepted, but his father discovering it made him spit them out on to the upchurned field. Then he was locked into the car as a real punishment. I did nothing. He says he forgives me but I doubt it. I would say that he was disappointed and rightly so in my lack of gumption. He developed gumption quite early on, and demonstrated it by scratching the paint off the lavatory seat when he was interned in there one afternoon to alter the course of his constipation. He just scratched the new turquoise paint off the lavatory seat. By then we had moved to the city, or rather to the outskirts of London.

Our house faced a common that was divided up into a sporting pitch and a walking area. The walking area had converging cinder tracks. It was dullness personified. My son was about four and very active with sticks and stones, with anything that he considered weaponry. One afternoon I walked across that common and for some unaccountable reason looked back and saw that my husband was trailing me with his binoculars. I pretended to play hide-and-seek with my son. The silliest thing happened. My son took up a big forked stick and hit and harmed a strange child for no reason at all except that tribulation was in the air. At once voices were raised, suits were pressed, names and addresses were exchanged as the strange boy's father pointed to a mark on the left eye-lid of the howling child. I said it was an accident, as if that could help the situation. The more the boy howled the more fatalistic were the father's threats. And as we walked away from them he kept following and saying, 'Police, Police.' My son and I came home and sat in the dining-room waiting for it to be five o'clock, waiting for the children's television to come on. I shall never forget the way I examined the black and white squares of linoleum as if in a dentist's waiting-room, and in reality I was waiting for my husband's call, for his 'Would you come upstairs, please.' I went up to the bedroom. He turned the key in the door.

'Any more monkey business out of you and I will have you committed.' I had heard those words before, in fact heard them when I was poised to elope with him. Too ridiculous.

'There is no monkey business,' I said, as brazenly as I could.

'You will do as you are told,' he said. 'From now on I am master.'

'He is my son,' I said, foolish beyond belief to have brought into circulation the very nub and crux of the matter. For all we each wanted was that little child with his beautiful mop of ash-blond curls and his eyes that were like pools, so deep so pensive and so brown were they. I even used to have dreams, waking dreams, about tearing him in half dividing him between us both and now I was mad enough to bring into question the very subject we had shirked, the very reason for our daily nightmare.

'I will take him to New Zealand where you will not see him,' he said. A desert sprung up before my eyes, more loss.

'You will never,' I said and ground my teeth and he struck me a few times, and that's nothing spectacular except that I lose my senses at the slightest whiff of violence.

I lay back on the bed, probably whimpered, and some time after he went down, took my son for a walk and gave him a traffic lesson that went something like 'Main road. Big buses. Footpath. Safety. Situation. Mother send boy on to main road on to carriageway, father protect boy and teach boy footpath. Mother mad.' I was mad if to be mad is to be incapable and suddenly stunned and moving slowly and sullenly and mindlessly like some sick beast, to peel potatoes, to lay table for three, to fill the water jug, and put a saucer over it, to take the three ringed napkins out of their drawer and place them on the sideboard, to prepare family dinner. They came back chirpy enough. My son had seen a shooting star. His father congratulated himself for the little expedition and said they must go out oftener at dusk, they must enjoy life. My son crouched down to topple the brick edifice he had just made so that he would have an excuse to make another, and from the kitchen I looked through the little service hatch, saw the laid table, saw his father take off his cap, scratch the top of his head, replace the cap again, saw how wrathful he was, saw that there was no way of continuing, no way of explaining, stirred the sauce, removed the apron, hung it on the hood of the door and went quietly out of the house and down a hill where there was a police station. They only thing they could ask me was did he molest me. I found it fairly funny. I spent the night on some bench, a bit numb and unafraid. Next day I fetched my son from his school and he was manliness itself as he got up from the little desk after the teacher had called his name. His hands and mouth were coloured because of the crayons he had been using. We were going on a journey. That was what I told him. It was a short-lived journey, to a shop to buy a gun, to friends' houses to try and thrash it all out, here and there, but to no purpose. There was no money behind it or no strategy. I had to bring him back. It was nightfall and he ran from the gateway touching the box hedge, as was his habit. He clattered at the letter-box, not being able to reach the bell. His father gave him a royal welcome and he ran in. I stood on the threshold of a house whose spick and spanness had been my daily responsibility. I saw letters on a silver plate and wondered if they were for me, wondered but did not ask.

'I'll collect him tomorrow,' I said, and mentioned a church fete where we might go.

'Oh no you won't,' he said and took his leave of me very formally, and in triumph. He did some sort of bow as if he was offering me a garland.

'You realise you have severed your last rights as a mother,' he said.

'He's only back for the time being,' I said and I could hear our son do a lusty hip hip hooray inside.

'He's back,' his father said, then closed the door and knowing that I had a latch-key he took the precaution of bolting it from the inside. I pawed at the door. I knocked with my knuckles on the glass half, while also ringing the bell. I clattered at the letter-box just as my son had done and then daring to peer through I saw my husband on the inside and our eyes met. It was a most unnerving thing. His shone fiercely, and also he chuckled. Then he stooped down and lifted something up. It was the shotgun. I saw its cold grey muzzle and I heard him open the barrel and pop the cartridges in. There was nothing for it but to go away, to go out the gate and down the street, to become another woman and I did. No longer a wife, not yet penitent and not yet whore. A bit of all three.

Pity for wives waned in me then. I had relinquished the role. I need never make jam, or wash blankets or say as I heard a key in the door, 'Have a good day?' Perhaps I miss the hypnotising slavery of it. Wives became strangers to me, enemies. So much so that when Dee suggested we go to Cornwall I did not think of disloyalty. I thought he means to sleep with me. He was taking me there in order to take mood photographs. I don't know what connection there is between restoring pictures, and being photographed on the edge of a cliff but he seemed to want it. He booked the hotel, he put the vase of June roses in my room, he pressed me to eat the choicest things. We used to work very early in the mornings, to catch the dew so to speak, and then after lunch we would go our separate ways. On the third day I slept so late into the evening that when I came down I learned that he and his assistant had gone out to dinner. To a three-star joint I was told. The same, the self-same pang that attends desertion took hold of me and I could not breathe, nor speak, and everything started to become black and blotchy. Except that I told myself that it was always such a silly little thing, that it was a misunderstanding. I learned from the assistant that Dee had hung about the lobby and had asked if I had called down but did not dare disturb me because I had left a message not to be wakened. Yet the pang was twin to all those others, those terrible infantile rages at not having fun, not having friends, not having. I made the best of it. I sat in the dining-room and read *Notes From Underground*, but ate heartily and drank likewise. *Notes From Underground* was a cry from the dark unloosened zones but pain on paper does not alter our hunger for satisfaction. It might induce a tear or two, it might make us vow to be more

40

serious, even more alert but we still ask for the banana ice cream, we stir the coffee, we sway mentally from the nice effects of the wine, we gaze out of a bow window, we simulate a little cough, we fold the napkin, we get up from the table, we enjoy the waiter's deference and in a state of self-induced blur cross the room as I did, look at the souvenirs in the lobby as I did, resolve to buy cut-glass goblets as I did, and then stick one's head out the door as I did, to steal a glance at moon or stars. They were both there, in full splendour, and the wind had dropped so that not one leaf of the little ornamental maple tree stirred. It had three orange lights round its base and because of that and its stillness it looked artificial. I decided to walk along the beach for health's sake, and to kill time.

Something unexpected met my eyes. In a way it was untoward. Down there, the universe was a gauze of white. It was as if the gods had fashioned it, so eerie, so threaded and so dense was it. I had a sudden mad message to peel off my clothes and run like a maenad through it, to free myself. Shoes, stockings, black tunic and long black skirt were all peeled off and flung. I ran and ran, and hollered and hollered, and felt a pain in my windpipe that was soon followed by a sense of space as if it were a channel for any oddment to pass through. I ran towards the next village though I could not see its street lights, but I could guess its direction. Freedom, recklessness, these were the feelings my soul craved. But I suppose it was all just bravura. I do not know how long I ran, or whether I became enfevered through running, or whether I had drunk too much, but I was clamouring to earth and air when suddenly I turned round, saw a figure and called out in martial fashion, 'Who goes there?' I might have known. No ghost. Ghosts do not follow us to fuck us. Dee had found me and his kiss, I have to say it – as a sampler of kisses – was delivered from the crown of his head, down the length of his rigid body, to his canvas-covered toes. His groin settled itself over mine like a coverlet, and his cock though sideways was one with me as if poised to pass through. He was shy, said his assistant had gone in for a dip, and wouldn't you know it! We did not consummate then. I am happy to say we walked along hand in hand, surprised by the dense whiteness, wondering what had caused it – condensation or some other phenomenon. Yet when it came to the crunch he was as fugitive as any of the others. 'Get out of my life' seemed to be the anthem, the very same as if I was a louse, the same as if we'd never whispered, the same as if his body had not nestled into mine, the same as if our senses had not temporarily cleaved to delight. Yes, he killed it. Why do people want to murder a wholesome thing? Odd, that I should pose that question. Soon it will be at my own doorstep. Why did you murder this young boy, on the threshold of life, as I am certain they will put it. Yes, his wrenching youth and his glowing innocence will be stressed, in direct contrast with my depravity.

Dee said that I let out a very poignant little tweak after I came. But I did not come. Yet I may have let out a sound that clearly he misunderstood. Dee had a side to him that puzzled me, baffled me. He said how he loved to get up early, long before wife, and family, open the double doors of his lounge, step out into his tangled garden, and savour life before he was intruded upon by any one of them. That was the peak of his day, being alone before they descended on him. Once it seems he found a mushroom and grilled it before the family breakfast. Presumably he ate it alone. He was lucky that it was an edible rather than a poisonous one. Then, as he said, the *Huis Clos*, the Little Hell commenced. That little saga led me to assume that he would be both more relaxed and more attentive when wife and family were away. As they were the night we consummated. He was guilt incarnate. He wound his watch after arriving, said perhaps we should not, said that the telephone at which he was renownedly bad could at any moment ring in his vacated house. Luckily he did not bring his dog into it or I would have bucked. I asked how he had slept knowing that he had been alone the night before. Badly. Disastrously. Now comes the episode that baffles me since all the rest is wearyingly predictable. The Mouse Story. There had been a mouse in the room it seems and, not unsurprisingly, its scurry and its scratching got on his nerves. He waited for it to go to sleep thinking that a mouse like himself was a creature who slept at night and moved throughout the day. No such luck attended his vigil. The mouse not only scurried and scratched, the mouse also screeched. At three in the morning he got out of bed determined to catch it.

'With what?' I asked, thinking, a poker, a shovel, a shoe, a shoe-tree.

'With my hands,' he said and smiled and presently laughed. There was spite in his laugh.

'You would have caught it and killed it with your hands?' I asked.

'Yee. . .es,' he said.

'How?' I asked.

'Squeezed it to death.'

I looked at him and felt a bit puzzled, felt the outsideness of him being observed and judged by the outsideness of me, and yet we were conspiring to go to bed, and furthermore his hands were inside my dirndl skirt, stroking me wildly and I had already stretched his penis towards his left thigh and was enticing it until it had almost nosed its way through the white denim of his trousers. Yet we were pretending to ignore what we were doing to one another. I think he was getting cold feet. Anyhow I raised one of my supple legs and to his amazement placed it to one side of his neck and I heard him say the word exquisite, and I thought I would flummox him a bit by discussing politics, or the state of the world, or what colour paint or paper on his bedroom wall. Instead I heard myself ask him at what time he usually retired at night. He said it depended on the adrenalin and I knew that his reply implied a host of things – on whether he desired or detested his wife, on whether she desired or rebuffed him, on whether they had got drunk, on whether they had a cosy family evening as harmless as boiled milk, or on whether a furore ensued during which his wife was found pitching things. It is amazing the number of wives who fling things. So that in a sense while he was taking off my shoes, my stockings, my suspenders, and my light summer skirt, I was thinking of his marriage bed. How often, how deeply, how searchingly, how hurtfully, how ravingly, and how covetously have I not thought of marriage beds. The marriage beds of others, the covers, the series of covers, under which they lurk, the secrets and confidences that are imparted, bonds made, bonds broken, the ordinariness and, yes, the extraordinariness of it all.

It was the next day I received from him the peony roses, the bouquet dripping with remorse, the bye-bye blackbird bunch. That everything seems to have to end! Even this little room I won't see again. It hardly deserves description. My chief interest in it is who else it has housed and what has been their fate. In short is it a lucky room. It is a dump. The bed. The chair. The washbasin. The chamber pot and the hot pipes that are at best lukewarm. Like a room I have dreaded from long ago. Perhaps we foresee, perhaps we get hunches. I go to the interview room when my solicitor and my barrister come. I went there twice and sat in a big glass zone. Don't think I didn't think of Hart and the time when he was under surveillance. The bitterest bit is that he would understand all this and passing the glass window he would leave a little kiss on it, a moist X. I sat there among the potted ferns while the two men looked at me. God knows what they thought, but they were politeness itself and they were breezy. The barrister was the nicer of the two. He had a sense of humour. He said did I not feel that I was in a castle what with the dragons and griffins over the turrets and what with the imposing stone front. I said I hadn't noticed having arrived there at dusk. We spoke about practicalities. He told me that the trial was to be held in Norwich. I go there tomorrow in a police car and I will sleep in the police station, for the time being, that is. It will take two or three weeks, maybe. My bag is packed. He warned me about not saying too much and about making my answers as short as possible. In that way I may forestall bungling it. But as I see it there is no way out. He thinks differently. He says we have a nice judge, a fuddy dud. He has placed the thought in me that Hart may have attacked me and that I may have killed in self-defence. But I cannot lie . . . I cannot . . . Yet I may have to lie. He

45

keeps saying to leave it to him. There is no knowing what I may do. But I will never forgive myself if I lie. He lives in the country and has a big wood of badgers.

I see Hart's face dead. It floats before me. It is true that I wanted to hit it, but that was because of his monstrous audacity in dying. Also the colour was changing in it, the colour was being drained out of it. Within minutes after dying, his complexion was the torrid yellow of bamboo cane and I do not like that colour on a man, especially on a dead man. I remember so accurately what I did. I lifted his right hand to take his pulse and instantly dropped it. I pulled the coverlet over his face while smoothing out the wrinkles on the other side of the bed where I had lain. Then for a moment not admitting that he was dead I indulged myself, said it was a decoy, and obliged myself to think a spiteful thought about Dee, about the fact that the one time when we were together he would not get beneath the cover and I took that to mean his quick getaway and I was right. Imagine being just introduced to death and thinking such a fallow, such a heartless, such a pointless, such a selfish thought. I said Jesus to Hart. His eyes were scary. They were always eyes which had shock in them but now they were aghast. They were always eyes that were like beautiful shields between him and the outside world, instruments through which his brain peered. Now they were eyes that knew the worst. I took my shoulder bag, then my stockings with suspenders attached, and my frilled knickers and went outside to dress. I would say that I did these things with a wizard speed because it was no length of time before I was down the stairs and out.

46

I was devoid of thought except for the sheer practical one of bending down to tie two shoelaces, without staggering. Next thing I was in the nearby pub ordering a double whiskey. It was a workman's pub and I was the only woman there. It was there that I had these horrible visitations – I could see his eyes quite separate from his body, just eyes in the air and the food that was being fried in the nearby kitchen smelt like the most malodorous shit. Nothing to what followed. I tried to think consecutive thoughts such as, where should I go, what should I do, what would happen when they found him, but these thoughts were lorded over by his two eyes that had begun to bleed and the smell of the shit that was being fried in the kitchen that got into the back of my mouth. I went to the Ladies' to wash. I washed my hands, then my mouth then I shook some water into my bosom then I pulled my knickers down and as best I could splashed my private parts. I was convinced that quite soon I would be examined for evidence. Anyone could have come in but mercifully they didn't. There was no washcloth so I just had to crouch and splash myself and hope for the best. I forgot in my flurry that it is him they would examine and that my fingerprints, my mouth-print, my body print, lay upon him, indelibly and indisputably like ice upon a frozen pond. Had his soul left his body? Was he face to face with his maker? Had telepathy started to work and did his mother hear a death knock in her home in Kensington? Were they getting anxious at the theatre? All this while I splashed myself, then improperly dried myself with pieces of lavatory paper. It was oatmeal coloured and coarse.

'The understudy, the understudy,' I heard myself say to the dismal and blotched mirror of a little medicine cabinet that was half-nailed to the wall. I would go to the understudy's digs. He was called Eddy. Maybe that was my mistake but I kept reciting the pat phrase, 'The show must go on.' I came out crying and asked the young barman to get me a taxi. I drank, I don't know how many whiskeys but I know that much later that night I vomited so, I thought I would choke. That was in a railway station. Because once the show went on, and it was over and the others had trooped back to the house, I followed, and as I came in the hall door I heard them roaring, I heard all the girls roaring and I knew at once that I would have to skedaddle. The roaring and wailing instantly turned it into a corpse house. I hurried back to my hotel room to throw my belongings in a suitcase and make a phone call. I had in fact a rough arrangement to go to a castle to discuss if I could restore one of their pictures. When I rang them the secretary said that they would be pleased to see me. I did not even get in touch with my son as I feared he might smell my crime. In a matter of hours he and all the world had turned into dangerous enemies.

During the trial he will want to intervene, will want to say a thousand and one little solacing things about the lame dogs that I have helped or the serving women into whose baskets I would put wine or a head of cabbage as they left late on a Saturday night. As if that mattered. I try to make amends to him. I talk to him about his career and the paths that lie ahead. We are both shifty. I almost prefer the visiting day when he doesn't come. Then I can think about him, think to my heart's content.

We lay in bed once and though our walls did not adjoin I knew that he was weeping, slow quiet terse unsatisfying tears. His life had taken one of those turns for the worst and we had had a tiff. It was about sleep. The craving for sleep was something I had not then conquered. It was as if sleep herself were some sublime mother with arms who would enfold and protect me. After three or four nights without it or with mere snatches of it I would want to batter everything. It was the fifth of such nights and long after midnight he took to moving odds and ends up into the loft, since he was leaving next day to start rehearsals for the Festival in Edinburgh, the famous Festival where it all happened. He decided to move his baggage just as I had drifted off and wakening suddenly my dreams snapped and I got out of bed, met him in the hall and launched into a furious outburst. I think I said as much as 'leave home'. It was a quarrel in which I was saying everything and he was saying nothing. He just stood on the ladder in his pyjamas looking blanched.

'It is not a house for this sort of thing,' I said, and then retreated to my room making sure not to slam the door, not to dramatise. But of course when I lay down my heart was pounding and I saw the switch of my bedside lamp just waiting to be pressed on. How I pitied him. Knew that he was suffering, was missing the previous girl. Only that day I had come on a little box of his, had opened it and found there a lock of hair, a ring stone, and a flake of tobacco. Memories of her. He spoilt his girls. Once he went to the sales and bought twinsets for three of them. He was afraid to show me these purchases lest I grumbled about extravagance, but then during supper he did. He pulled them out of their cellophane wrappers, held them up to his chest and asked which I thought was suitable for which girl. Yes I knew I would have to go to him to apologise. Yet I tried not to. I remembered edicts about character formation. I thought 'The young never learn if one is not hard', and then I thought what gibberish and went directly to his room. He was snivelling.

'Down in the dumps?' I asked and he nodded. The girl he had broken off with kept coming back in his thoughts. She was in Tunisia with another boy and had even sent cards, jolly cards.

'Jocasta?' I said, daring to pronounce her name. I had never fully liked her.

'You might become reunited?' I said, because I loved him enough to want anything for him.

'It's not that,' he said. 'It's just, regrets.'

And I knew that he had absorbed something that I was still striving for. He had learnt the inevitable: 'What's done is done, what's dead is dead.' Yet he too knew that nothing is utterly dead and the departed leave in us an invisible gong that can strike at any moment. He was in need of a cigarette and asked if I had any hidden for him. I used to hide them and surprise him by hauling them out from behind a cushion or from inside a cup. But that night I had none. He said he would make do with miming a smoke. He mimed lighting it, then having the first three hearty inhalations, in a quick row, then a long exhalation, then an automatic tip onto an imaginary ashtray, then the next satisfying puff and so on and on until we were both certain we saw smoke in the room, and he even went so far as to blow smoke rings out. The desire became so great that he dressed, went off on his bicycle and got a packet from a machine. We sat up for most of the night, talking.

'I didn't give you enough of my time this hols,' he said. It was his reverting to the word hols that anchored most of all, as when a grown person says blissikins or lovikins and you cannot keep a dry eye.

'You will come to the Festival,' he said and I said maybe, not knowing what it would lead to. He always had a soft heart. He saw a tramp pick up orange rinds, and then drop them again in disgust and he was so disturbed that he was unable to offer the tramp the coin he would have liked to give. You could say he was impotent with sheer despair.

The night before the court his father had asked him to sign a letter to tell the judge what was his intention in life as regards parental custody. He was put in a room with pen and paper, even a spare sheet of paper lest he blot or make a mistake. His father had heated a pot of sealing wax and dangled a bit of it on the end of the rubber spatula, one I used to use for getting the dough out of the bottom of bowls while I was still an exemplary housewife. His father recommended that he write the correct thing which was to renounce Mother who was mad, being a woman, and to espouse Father who was good and upright, being a man. But he did not see it that way. He wrote: 'Dear Dad, No doubt I will want to be with you later for shooting and fishing and hunting etcetera but just now I would like to be with my Mum.'

Vengeance has caught up with us. There remained this heavier destiny. He will go through life with this smear, this horror. To others the case will smack of juiciness. People will look at it as that of a young boy and a passionate older woman but it was more than that. There will be photos of Hart. He will be likened to the ear of corn that the scythe cut down. His beauty will be remarked upon, condoned, his long Christ-like face, his soft shoulder-length hair and his mouth like the lips of a beautiful purse that opened wide in order to be deployed of its contents. I knew in advance that when it came to loving his mouth would shower me with kisses. I had no idea that we would be so well matched except that we were. Uncanny. His mouth found mine unerringly in the dark and we had each conceived the same thoughts at the same moment.

Being kissed by him had in it all the freshness and innocence of a spring day. Yet there was in it too an intoxication. The spring would pass and the drugged madness of autumn would come. Except that we never arrived there. Kiss upon kiss upon kiss. Impossible to count them. It's all a dream now. His death a dream too. One thing does rack me, one query – did he know that I was actually killing him, and how many seconds were there between his knowing and his expiring, and in that time what thoughts did he think, and if he were to come back to life would he curse me or hunt me down or would he, as I hope, forgive. A black man cursed me once in a department shop. I was buying or rather endeavouring to buy a spare part for a washing machine and not being mechanical I was hopeless at trying to describe it. The lengths he went to help me! He showed me new machines, put the motors on and I must say seeing them working so smoothly, their surfaces unsullied, tempted me to chuck economy and buy a new one. The salesman said 'Nonsense', that we would get the old one working like new. But I could not tell what was broken. He drew various parts and still I shook my head from side to side and eventually he decided that a man from the works had better call and inspect it. Putting his pencil behind his ear and assuming a very cavalier stance he picked up an internal telephone, asked for Service and said he had a lady who was having trouble with her washing machine then passed on the name and address and said, 'Mark it urgent.' Then came the tally-ho. He said what was I doing that evening and when I evaded he pressed with an invitation and when I said 'No', he pointed two long pink-tipped fingers in the direction of my eyes and said 'Oooba dooba' with such ferocity that I thought my vision was being plucked from me. I thought at once of my mother and of her ingrained irrational fear of black magic. In fact her vision of reaching heaven is severely marred by the fear, that all those savages whom missionaries have converted will be strolling around walk-in the gardens, sitting on the deck chairs, using cups and goblets, availing of baths and lavatories if there are such amenities there. I reckon she puts veils on them, white, all-enveloping veils. She passed on to me that trait and a bit of a craving for finery. Prison smocks do not thrill me, nor do sensible shoes. She got a coat once on approbation and you would think it was hers for life. For one thing she hung it up in the wardrobe, indeed stripped the wooden hanger of the six or seven garments that were somehow cleaving to it. It was Persian lamb with a big cape collar. The collar as she said, would make a coatee for me. She decided to keep it. She even removed the price tag and placed it in the bone box on the bureau where jewellery was stored; jewellery being nothing more than cheap tangled necklaces, and a string of artificial pearls. Yet she would have it that these pearls were seed.

The coat was worn three times, twice to mass, and once to evening devotions. Soon after it was folded, put back in its important cardboard box, tissue paper tucked neatly around it and the brown paper that covered the box turned inside out to carry the new address. The inside-out paper did not have the same sheen at all. It was coarser. She wrote the address and dispatched the parcel with considerable stoicism. She said years later that she wouldn't give tuppence for Indian lamb or Persian lamb or any of those crazes but at the time she would have bartered anything to keep it. Getting it on approbation was, in my mind, tantalisation and error. It was like a visitor who came for an hour or two. We liked visitors, perhaps we thought they would bring us tidings like the Magi or better still that they would waft us away to happier far-off places.

We hid from some. We hid from drunkards. My father had cronies, fellow-topers who in their cups sought out his company. They would arrive at any hour and he would go outside to speak with them and he would not come back. Once when she had gone on a day pilgrimage they stole the cut glasses to drink from. They took them across the fields. She found them on the headland of a ploughed field with not a chip on them.

'Like angels,' she said, picking them up as if they were jewels or turkey eggs and then she smelt them and made a face. The smell of drink turned her stomach, as did childbirth, black-magic and hearsay concerning couples who met in the woods. In fact all forms of cavort sickened her stomach. She and I were happy only on those rare days when we were alone, and her husband was being weaned off drink by temperate monks who led him around a close reciting a chain of prayers, in order to receive a plenary indulgence, and seek the grace to turn over a new leaf. She and I would clean the house

54

from top to bottom, the balls of fluff under beds would be scooped out with a wing, the mattresses would be turned, sheets changed, bolsters beaten so that the flock was not in knots beneath, soot swept from under all the fireplaces, wax applied to all the floors and all the surrounds, a finer wax put on the leafed mahogany table, the silver dipped and then polished until each surface was like a mirror to peep into, windows cleaned on both sides, and then draped with snow-white, or cream-white, lace curtains that fitted snugly against the pane itself.

The way I see it now, I think we were cleaning our souls when we did such a thorough job of our abode, cleaning our souls of all our sins, mortal and venial. But her sin in her eyes and her sin in my eyes are a matter for dispute. I have never really tackled her and my mind bends under the weight of accusations that I have not voiced. She went to him, her butcher husband, she went on command. She who objected to intimacy. She appears to have known no pleasure and perhaps given none. Pleasure. That incendiary word.

I tried to cast her off but it was not easy and it was not possible. It was as if she'd already lodged in me, was interred in me, and she is interred in me now. Creature. I would think of occasional and random things like gathering crab apples with her, or the way she scoured a saucepan, or clapped her hands together to imprison a fly, or the one time I saw her succumb. Those thoughts or rather those images would not quit me. Perhaps I did not want to be rid of her. Yet I did want. It was like the step of a dance that I ached to master but could not.

I relived it, that blundering awkwardness with Hart. He tried to show me how to swing from a bar, in a children's playground. I failed to do it. He lifted me up and told me the chest muscles that were involved, but mine were helpless and would not move. Yet it was *her* crippledom that prevented me. I re-enact it now, I even fancy I can do it, for Hart. I climb on the window-sill, put my hands up on the frame and swing from it. Each time the paintwork cracks just another little sliver. I tell myself that if I do it he is perhaps not dead, and that is worst. I see him sidle across a room, his beautiful half-guarded, dark, mauve-brown eyes ready to smile at whatever crops up.

The first night he stayed in my house he slept alone, downstairs on a sofa that converted into a bed. In the middle of the night he had occasion to get up. I expect nature called, but being fastidious he said he had needed a glass of water. Then on coming back into the room he could not find the light switch and he became convinced that there was a ghost there. He was also convinced that the ghost occupied the space between him and the edge of his bed, and, as he so quaintly put it, he sidled across the room and slipped into bed and was safe. I do believe he desired me then, expected me perhaps to appear in a loose-fitting gown with ashes of roses on the temples but I did not presume. I lay upstairs, two floors up, congratulating myself on my reserve and on my virtue. I would not go to him, I would not compromise him, not lower myself, not dismay my son, though he slept like a top despite a vociferous alarm clock. I knew how transitory these things are. Take Dee. Take that moonlight walk and all the other preparatory things. Yet eventually – which is to say three or four or five weeks later – when we did make love, he asked as he was unwinding the laces of my mulattos if in fact we ought to. A damper across the face you might say. I lay down full of the memory of the impossible and Dee lay down full of I don't know what – cares possibly. I thought that he might exactly imitate my former lover, Jude, that a spirit might guide him, but no, he was brusque, and without tenderness and something expired in me. He said to close my eyes and breathe as if it was my first time. In a way it was, it always is. Afterwards he asked me what my week was like and I felt so separate. My week did not have much to it. When he got up he made mention of a whimper of mine that he would always think of as being poignant. But the things that could have been said were not. Not 'I care', or 'I like', or 'I fear', nothing at all. Perhaps he did not want attachment. He said what he feared was my anger but this was before my anger had been given any rein. He was in great haste as he availed of the potato soup and the various hot dishes I had prepared. His mother and Jude's had the same name as mine, the same christian name; the vital link.

THERE WILL COME a moment down there when the prosecution will ask me why. Why did you kill this man? I can hear everyone including myself wait for this terrifying reply.

'I lost my head my lord', or 'I had a brainstorm', or 'It gave me power', or 'It was unintentional', or 'I punished him for the sins of others'. Frankly, have I not always had a secret desire to kill. Have I not lived day and night wanting to kill the father who sired me, the father, scion of all fathers, who soiled my mother's bed, tore her apart, crushed her and made her vassal. Was I not sucked down into her darkest chambers, the witness and nursemaid of her mental and physical haemorrhaging. Did she not implore me to save her from this vale of woe? As if I were able. I think she confiscated my lungs too. I think that she is in full possession of my respiratory system. As it happens she is raving now. In the death throes, so she will not be able to give her appalled and fertile disapproval to my deed. She will not know that I have paid in her chosen coin for one of life's little sweetmeats – that I am condemned. I would pity her if only I did not have to pity her. When she dies, as I believe is imminent, she might meet Hart and they might confer about me, toss matters over. I imagine a little moment with her voice at its most conspiratorial as she asks him 'Did she commit sin?', and Hart will probably say 'No' although in those last minutes he did comprehend the monstrosity of what I was doing and I doubt that he forgave. Can I say that I forgive her? No. A resounding no. But come to think of it have I not always wanted to kill her too? Oh my God I have said it. She whom I loved like a litany, she to whom I said secular prayers, the features of whose face I have carried before me like a medallion, like an image of beauty, an image of hope, the guarantee of love, the shield, the buffer between me and all that is wicked and all that dies and all that rots. What ferocity. What we demand of mothers. Except that we do. The moment that she sensed in me affection for another she was serpent-like. Take the very last day, with Jude, when she showed her true colours. I saw her no more than once a year but luck would have it that I was in her company the day of its demise. The blackness, the waste and the futility of it all came to flower on a teeming afternoon. I was with her and I enlisted a friend, a Tom, to ring Jude at his house and ask that he ring me. No sooner had I made the phone call than I felt deliriously happy. I felt relief was nigh. I walked into one of those downstairs rooms that I know from childhood and that are impossible to banish from my mind's furnishing. But to pass a few moments before re-hearing his voice I went in there and roamed. I touched the ornaments, the china and the plaster ornaments, remarked on what a good sheen there was on the silver, counted the bottles of lemonade laid on their sides into a disused coal scuttle, sat by the window displaying exemplary patience when all of a sudden the telephone rang in the opposite room. It had quite a different, a more alerting ring than the phone I was used to, and I went in with alacrity. It was Tom.

'All is well,' he said. My heart toppled with relief. He had talked to Jude in person, was kindly received, had conveyed the message as to where I was, and now it was a mere question of time before he telephoned.

During lunch I rallied, praised my mother's cooking and gulped sweet sherry in between eating pieces of lamb chop, accompanied by dollops of mashed potatoes. As always she overfilled my plate and when I objected she exemplified a kind of mock anger to hide her real anger, and enjoined me to cut out the nonsense. Was I still afraid of her? Yes and no. But chiefly I did not want to spoil what was, after all, going to be a happy day, a day of reunion, when love returns to itself like a homing bird, and the two people say the expected words and re-find the trust that was briefly and capriciously lost. After we had washed up I soaked the dishcloths in a white disinfectant and begged her to lie down. No, she would not rest, there was some sinfulness attached to resting.

I had to visit an old Colonel in connection with my work and afternoon was the best time in which to do it she said. It seems he retired early and was usually drunk by night. Yes she would answer the phone. Suspecting the worst, which is to say suspecting something amorous, she was a little tart. As always when I stood on the doorstep about to leave she resorted to a Yankee accent and said, 'Have a noice time.' I was almost pleased to be going out, to give a little extra edge to Jude's flounder when he did ring.

My son drove. The drive brought to my mind Gogol's *Dead Souls*. It was pelting. The rain was torrential. To say it rained is not a way to depict things. Sheets of water fell from the heavens, parts of the road were like lakes that we splurged through; the windscreen wipers crawled in their efforts, so great was the load of water they had to push aside. Oars would have been more suitable. The one pedestrian we passed gave the appearance of a tent so weighed down with raincoats was it. It stopped. It carried a bucket. It looked as if it was going nowhere. We too had gone astray. My son drove with a recklessness that I think was imparted to him by the elements and by my agitation. He laughed a lot, outrageous laughter; that, for him, was a bad sign. As we crossed a bridge we saw the stones of one of its walls shake and knew it was on the point of toppling over. I wondered, not unnaturally, if it was raining as badly three counties hence where Jude lived. I envisaged his journey to the telephone kiosk – a journey he would have to execute with immense caution – and I did him the favour of putting a coat over him, one of those long oilskins in a becoming shade of dark green. For although he had brown eyes there was in them somewhere, far from sight, a layer of dark green. My son drove up any avenue that he saw and then as the puddles deepened would at once decide that it did not lead to the Colonel's decaying home. Once he got out to open a gate and lost his sombre black hat in the gales. It was quite amusing to see him dash across the fields after it and stumble on the mounds of grass. By the time he finally caught up with it and succeeded in grasping it – he had caught up with it once or twice before but missed his clutch – it was as wet and unlovely as the dishcloths I had put to soak. Momentarily he was vexed with me and vexed with life. I took it on my lap and said it would dry out, and we would restore its shape and that in fact the rain would help to give it character. I did not want a quarrel. I wanted his support.

At the next gateway, which is to say the next construction of wrought iron held together with barrels, barbed wire, bits of carpeting, a big speckled dog bared its teeth and the gatekeeper came out of her cottage and told us to be off.

'Ye're lucky Captain didn't ate the legs off ye,' she said, doing nothing to stall him as he edged his way between a hole in the gateway. We rushed back to the car and once in there I wanted to throw an implement at him and his mistress. We reversed up to the main road and mindlessly took a right turn. It was a tarred road and looked as if it led to somewhere. The rain had got worse, the world was blinding, and I was starting to have terrible presentiments. Coming towards us in the distance was a tinker's cart. We recognised it by its shape, by the fact that the pony was piebald, and by the recklessness of the driver. He commanded the middle of the road, was a youth of about twenty-five with scalding red hair and a cloth cap that was soaking. We had to pull in to the side and slowing down we shouted out to him and asked if he knew where Colonel So-and-So lived. He took one quick look at us and instantly a spout of curses emitted from him – 'Ye shit, shite, goddammed fucking sons of bastards, may ye roast in hell.' Then he lashed the pony and was off at a fantastic speed. The woman who was in the back of the cart raised her fist to us and I said to my son for God's sake to drive on lest they assault us. He swerved out on to the middle of the road, lost his bearing for a moment, then he too set off at a speed that was not only reckless but imitative of the tinker. We were both shouting at one another, and he pitched the vehicle forward although he could not see the way. I thought this will lead to disaster and yet I went on railing at him.

At the next cross-roads I had recovered some kind of equilibrium and asked him in God's name to slow down. I got out of the car. It was as if the countryside was hit by deluge. Sheets of water covered the fields. I walked a few yards and saw a painted sign which carried half of the lettering of the house we had been looking for. The avenue, of course, was rutted and the grass between the tracks had not been scythed or not been mown throughout the summer. It took the car all the power it had, to mow and muster its way towards the two-storied stone house on a hill. Most of its slates were gone. To the left of it was a caravan, with a barrel of water underneath a spout. That was where the Colonel lived.

We were cagey about getting out, and made a lot of noise in case there was another speckled dog. We hoped that he would present himself at once and enable us to dart back to the safety of the car. Then we would blow the horn to alert the Colonel. No animal slooped out, and it was not surprising since nothing would venture out on such a day, unless compelled to. We went up the steps of the caravan and held on to each other both from fear and because they were slippery. I knocked with wet knuckles on the glass half of the door. I knocked several times and the knocking increased in impertinence, in direct ratio to my sinking despair. 'Not in,' my son said and then all of a sudden from inside the caravan a telephone started to ring. Ting-a-ling, a-ling. I swear in my heart and I believe it to this day that it was Jude ringing me, that it had to be Jude considering the intuition we both shared. I would have broken into the caravan but that my son restrained me.

'No, Nora, no.' He calls me by my name when he wants to impress something serious upon me. He calls it to me here, when he is advising me to eat.

'No, Nora, no.'

We loitered in the rain for a few more minutes and then went back to the car and put the heater on. Our clothes were steaming and our faces as wet as if we had plunged them into barrels of water. I could not stop crying. It was as fecund as the rain. My son said what could he do. He just did not know. The welter of tears seemed to confound him. I remembered that in the village, as we slowed down to let cattle pass I had seen a notice about a faith healer who was in the next big town and I wondered if we could go there. He said certainly. He was the soul of solicitude. He would have driven the car through the slate quarry if it promised to make the grief less. And so we went.

There was an odd coincidence. The faith healer was not unlike Jude, the same beard, the same religious eyes, gravity mixed in with boyishness. Like the others I knelt before him. I would be obliged to say what my ailment was. I heard others say shingles, or catarrh or rheumatism and I felt twinges of shame and guilt. I felt pity for them as I knew they could not feel pity for me. When it came to my turn I said 'Private'. What must he have thought! He looked me in the eye and for one fleeting berserk moment I was hoping that he would kiss me. I felt a kiss of his would alter the flow of my luck. He put his hands on my shoulders and then I prayed. I prayed, though there was no enjoinder to pray. It was a temporal occasion. Yet when we came out I felt twinges of hope again. I thought now that the worst was over as indeed it was. My son had brought me a whiskey and the two of us sat in a little alcove admiring the deep rich ambers of the whiskeys in their glasses, and the old-fashioned water jug that bore the name of a brewers, long since defunct. I spoke to Jude in my mind and said that if he had ever loved me, then in the name of that love, even as a relic of that love, to ring me and say that at least we were friends and that the link was not broken. My life depended on it as did the balance of my mind. I knew that it had only not to happen, for blackness, madness, jangle and lunacy to take charge of me again. But I knew he would, even that he had already rung.

By the time we set out for home, the rain had ceased and as we drove through the country there were a profusion of rainbows. They were everywhere like scarves flung on the inky sky. People had come out of their houses and their cottages, gardens were fresh, the begonias and sweet williams seemed twice as bright. It was milking time and as we stopped to let cows go by we waved to people and they waved back and the world did not seem so be nearly so deserted. The herd of white cows belonging to the spinster woman were grazing as always on the roadside, stark white they were except for the black tips to their horns. I described her puckered face, the black kerchief on her head, the assortment of jumpers she wore and her reply when questioned by the police about her stray cattle. She always feigned distress, said she had roastings in her head. Perhaps she had. We laughed. He enjoyed going through the puddles. We bought fruit and tinned things at a new supermarket, and I bought wine with which to celebrate.

First thing my mother said was 'No messages'. I felt she was pleased. We unpacked the bits of shopping and as always seeing delicacies she said it was extravagance.

I uncorked the wine and took a big swig before going to the china cabinet to get a stemmed glass. She watched me drink and pretended that she did not disapprove. Her opprobrium was in full sway. To her such a phone call was only a prelude to whoring and not to receive it God's blessing.

At nightfall I rang my friend Tom and since there was no news I asked him to try again. He seemed disappointed in me. I waited in the room where the phone was and kept touching things, to divert the panic. I felt each surface for its inlay of dust, not that I cared about dust. In all, the matter took about fifteen minutes. Tom rang back and he was extremely blunt.

'No go,' he said.

'What?' I said.

'He wouldn't speak to me,' he said.

'Who spoke?'

'His wife spoke. 'He was definitely piqued.

'And?'

'He was too busy.'

'When will he speak?'

'Never,' he said.

I think I let out a shout after I had thanked him and replaced the heavy black dusty speaker. I must have, because instantly she was there to witness my outburst.

'All this crying gets one nowhere,' was what she said. Soon there would be scenes of reproach or supplication, scenes which her mistrust of liaisons would make her fluent in. Soon there would be questions, a post-mortem and a pledge never to get in touch with him again. I hurried out of the room and upstairs to lie on a bed, to

67

wallow. Later my son came up with the remains of the wine. She had questioned him, had cross-examined him. She had said to him, 'This thing your Mother is crying over, is she at fault?' He and I sat on the bed, and with one hand he held on to mine, and with the other fingered the little chenille buds on the bedspread. I said to him that I would have to go, that I could not stay, that I detested the place, but he begged me to wait till morning.

'I can't, I can't,' I would say.

'It's only ten hours,' he would say.

'I can't,' I repeated and he would squeeze my hand or fiddle with another of the little chenille roses on the bed-spread. Somehow we got through the night and left on a false pretext in the morning.

'You went to the Festival of Edinburgh.'

    'You booked into such and such a hotel.'

    'You took out a grey army blanket.'

    'You ran a bath.'

    'You put a photograph on your dressing table.'

    'You were called to the telephone.'

    'You left the hotel.'

    'You returned with the deceased to collect a grip-bag.'

These words boomed through me and even in sleep I hear them, each sentence preceded by the fall of a mace.

It is a funny thing how quickly one changes character, or rather one is changed. I used to see programmes on television in which murderers were being sought out and it amazed me that on those programmes they could tell exactly what time the unfortunate victim came in the door, what door he came in, how many shots were fired, where the bullets lodged, where he collapsed. It was the kind of programme that had nothing to do with me. I still believe it hasn't. I still believe that mine was different. Hart would vouch for it. I used to have to waken him in Edinburgh and always as I bent over him he would flinch, then smile. The blue sleeping bag that served as an eiderdown would have slipped down to the side and faithful to modesty I would cover him over and he would smile. Does he think it is another I would instantly think. But no. Even in sleep he registered quickly and said my name. He will be the last, the very last to inhabit my thought and that is something. Shall I tell them that or shall I say happiness is shortlived? I do not know what I shall say and as it gets nearer it seems to me that I will be able to make no sense at all, that I will say incomprehensible things, gibberish, even obscenities. There is no knowing when one is cornered.

I do not want to strike them as a crazed woman. Neither as a Dame Dora. Nor seek pity. Let pity not be dragged into it. And for a very sound reason: I still do not think that I was wicked. Rash maybe, and racked by the impossibility of a fruitful love, and chiefly putting my own cause before that of another. But killing him was an aberration. It was not a crime. He was the last person I wanted to kill. I wanted him alive for us, for happiness, for cuddles, for the few years before I began to fade. Of course I foresaw some of the difficulties. At odd moments if it suddenly thundered or if a highly strung Abyssinian cat crossed our paths or we had a lovers' quarrel I jumped ahead to a future time, his departure, the throes, trying to get him back. I knew that I would eventually have to imagine being without him, being deprived, but for the most part those fears were in abeyance.

Wherever I go, wherever I am sent, I expect I will be on good behaviour and what will that do – shorten my term by a few years. I have no inkling of the future except that I suppose I will be let out one distant day and feel estranged like one of those mourners who arrive at a funeral too late. I was a visitor once in an institution and I remember seeing all the women in groups doing hand-work and there were pools of pee under some of their chairs. The warders chain-smoked. I'd gone there to talk about my work. The women showed not a flicker of interest, why should they.

Yes there are times when I vehemently curse him, curse Hart. Why didn't he stop me? Why didn't he defend himself? Why doesn't his saint soul see to it that I am abducted from here, this very instant and brought if necessary to scorching Australia. I have played that little game again and again. I am sitting here, on the floor, cross-legged, alternating the cross of the legs when the door opens and I see not the henna-haired female guard but a masked man who reveals himself as a friend. He picks me up, he steers me down the hallway, he stuns the guards, he puts chloroform on the dogs, we cross the courtyard, I see a ladder by the light of a moon, he helps me up and on the other side is a voice that says, 'Now what do you think of that.' Freedom, hills, stars, nature; I get carried away.

I shall miss nature. The meadows, the cowslips so gold

like an abundance of rings, the newborn calves sunning themselves and the gnats in a haze all about their eyes. I shall miss the birds piping, the farm machinery, the rhododendrons as they budded, as they bloomed and finally as they wilted; the dark chocolate earth beneath the bushes and at nightfall the crackle of twigs as animals moved about. And my friends, the ones that hardly spoke at all, the others who spilt their hearts out. I dare not think of those hours, those full hours as darkness fell, as friendships were reinforced and suddenly one jumped up and said it was time to light a lamp or time to make a cup of tea. I shall miss men despite the sorrow they caused. I shall miss my own house with its pictures and its soft lamps and a peculiar smell of incense that it seemed to give out. The last party that I gave there was the one in which the ceiling fell in. Perhaps that too was a sign. It was three in the morning and a visiting labrador dog lay sprawled across the stairs, chewing his young mistress's knickers. It was a black little affair with lace edging. I stepped over him to get to the kitchen where I knew there lay in a saucepan new potatoes, browned in butter and flavoured with mint. I shared them with him. Quickly he discarded the knickers and waited for each new potato while I masticated mine. The party had gone off wonderfully. The songs sung had sent spells of joy through the guests and one had induced a chill. A woman sang it:

> You took the east from me
> And you took the west from me
> You took the sun and you took the stars from me
> Great is my fear love, you took God from me.

The whole room became hushed, chatting couples became very pensive, the man with the guitar dropped his head, the dog panted. A second after she had finished and while the applause was still issuing someone asked if perhaps she would sing it again. She did. The window was wide open and I could hear people halt in their footsteps and say, 'Ssh' to one another as they stood and listened. All in all it was remarkable – the whole room hushed, people in the street stopping in their tracks, and a smell of honeysuckle everywhere. Then the doorbell rang. I was convinced it was Jude. I was as convinced as that the song had just ended, that glasses were being refilled, that the candle flames were moving to the merest draughts and that each flame held a shifting cone of blue. I was as convinced as that. It was in fact Jude's birthday and the party was held for him as if by intuition he would know. There he was ringing the doorbell just before midnight, like heroes in legends, arriving, just in the nick of time. How I preened as I drew back the latch. It was a stranger to ask if he might come in. I said yes, not knowing how to say no. He might have been a murderer! Ah how unselective I was then. He was a philosopher or so he said. He wore jeans and bright two-toned baseball boots. I believe he was American. I introduced him as the Philosopher. He never opened his mouth again, just nodded as the songs were being sung, or as a heated argument developed as to whether George fucking Bernard Shaw was a tactician or a playwright.

Then at about five as I ate and relished the cold potatoes the ceiling fell in. I heard its thud, and then bits of clutter and when I went in tongues of plaster hung from the ceiling and the parquet floor was strewn with white. For some reason I laughed, and when my son came down to see what had occurred he found me squatting on the floor like someone heartened at finding herself in a shambles. I said that I never wanted the night to end. It was as if I had suspended pain, loneliness and dread, and much more so it was as if all these things were way behind me. He allowed me to caress his bare insteps, and stroke his toes. We knew each other by heart, the slightest tiff, the merest tear, a bubble of desire was understood mutually by both of us and when I see him now I see how he is also living my plight. He is ashen and he puts on a façade of manliness, so as to hide his upset. He almost chokes. Just before he leaves he takes my elbow and says everything will be all right. In those moments I want to hit him.

I WONDER IF the sights of Tuscany will help me through. I saw so many pictures of martyrdom, St Johns of all countenances, Popes, innumerable Christs stretched across windows urging mankind to repent. Altars so decked and so profuse with flowers it was as if gardens bloomed beneath them. Frescoes too. Those that depicted scourging and those that depicted happy domestic scenes. Then a painting of a little girl whom death claimed because she had taken an apple from a stranger. They are so fresh in my mind, they are perhaps my buffer in this heartless room. In fact sometimes I have been able to imagine myself back there, particularly seeing those paintings on a yellow wall, on a summer's day; paintings in which the actual figures were so faint that at times one saw them, at other times they vanished. In short they came and went like spirits, like shadows. Yet they were perfect as was the long dining-room with its round arches and the verandah scorchingly bright being packed with pots of geraniums. Beyond the railings there was a drop to a valley of green impassive trees.

Soon after the tea and the buckwheat pancake, I was invited to go to Tuscany to restore some pictures. Hart and my son had gone to Edinburgh to start rehearsing a play. I was glad to leave and yet I had such apprehension about my journey. My future employer was a millionaire and a bit peculiar. He was a falconer and more interested in his hawks and in the tame birds he fattened for them than in his collection of paintings. My friend Madeline had arranged it. She had taken a villa next to his for the summer.

Ours was a chartered flight and we were all crammed in together. It was very boisterous and soon I forgot my apprehension. When we landed most of the passengers clapped. They were workers going home to Italy and somehow they were amazed at the miracle of a plane landing. Later I boarded a train and followed one side of the Apennines and watched them alter in bulk as the light faded. They seemed to grow larger. They were dark and beautiful, cleft in places and in other places pointed where a high ridge must have jutted up. They gave authority and mystery to the scene that flat land never does. Perhaps there were many mountains all of different colours and having different heights and different peaks but in the dark, and seen from a distance, they seemed like one vast silent presiding giant. It was a pleasure to be there. A strange boy sitting opposite me, who amused me by stretching his limbs, by proffering cigarettes, by a frequency of smile, in short by manifests of desire. He even touched the hem of my dress to comment on its being couture. I had a quarter bottle of wine, and we shared it, each of us being very careful to wipe the mouth of the bottle before passing it back. I expressed a longing for a piece of bread and saucily he added to my hunger by suggesting bits of sausage, salami, then slices of cured ham, and figs. I would look up the words in the dictionary, smile and almost salivate as I translated each one. There is no doubt that he courted me.

It was an express train and every so often he would hold up his watch to show me that we were getting nearer and nearer to Florence. He was disappointed that I was being met although he himself was engaged and getting married the following month. Where was she? Preparing her bottom drawer, I imagined. The night air and the strangeness of the countryside gave excitement to my journey.

At the station, though, there was a little incident that shook me. A young woman, almost a girl, was carried away by two carabinieri and throughout she shouted back to someone in the station restaurant. Maybe she was shouting to any one of us. I could not understand the words, but her outrage frightened me and I too thought that I might instantly begin to scream. I have not screamed here yet. I have not wavered, I am holding on to life, as to a thread. It is terrifying.

Off they carted her, and now the shouts, not nearly so penetrating, came to us through the air. Then silence.

As soon as my friend Madeline came I felt settled. We drove out of the city and then deeper and deeper into a mountain pass. I shall never forget it – the strangeness of the landscape, a fragrance of the various trees, hilltops and valleys. There was a half moon, the sky was serried with stars and the valleys were mysterious oases in which there were vine and olive orchards. We would pass a farmhouse that seemed fast asleep, a hulk of sleeping stone with only its watchdog on the alert. At intervals single or even groups of cypress trees loomed up and they were like big dark question marks giving particularity and peculiarity to the whole.

When we got to the villa there was a heavy mist and we had to link as we groped our way from the car. She was disappointed that I could not see anything. Inside a fire blazed, a tray was laid for drinks, and all at once life seemed pleasant and ordained. In the salon were five or six young boys, two of whom were playing backgammon, and I said to myself – daftly – my future is pregnant with young men. Little did I know.

In my bedroom I thought of Hart, of his being there, somehow I thought I had stolen him in, that he had climbed in the window and was hiding. I saw that smile. His delight in things was unique. He would for instance hold a postcard up to the light and look at it and marvel at it. God only knows what he would have done had he seen a Giotto painting, had he seen the throats of those men, those Jobs, who have the capacity but not the authority to let out an indefinite scream. He would have seen his own predicament.

I recall my room in the villa, every aspect of it. It was sparsely furnished and that is a good thing because I can summon it up in a minute and there is no clutter. There was the big bench next to the wall, where I put my clock and my toiletries, and where there was already a container of insecticide in case of midges. Midges. It rained all the time at first, so that even they went into hiding.

There was an old round hall stand and on to each of the wooden prongs I flung some of my clothing, so that anyone entering the room would immediately assume that it was a stage prop so decked was it with scarves, purses and multi-coloured dresses. No one did enter the room except the maid each morning with a flask of coffee, warm bread, and three flavours of jam. I would ask her not to open the shutters because I hate being sighted when I waken and also it was sweeter to lie in the dark, and sip the coffee and take the crusts of bread and dip them in the variety of jams and honey. Invariably she forgot a knife.

Then at last when my eyes were ready for it I got up and undid the shutters. The catches on one pair were iron and the little oiled bolt slid back and forth like a dream as if it were waiting for that, as if that were its only desire. I would do it several times for amusement, its own and mine, and then suddenly throw the shutters outwards and there the world would be and there the leaves wet, shivering, and hushed. The olive leaves would be silverish, and the others various hues of green or yellow and as far as the eye could see were these trees and the dark cypresses, the blurs of black, beside the yellow stone houses with red shingled roofs. Even the telegraph poles seemed rustic in among the trees. They were small wooden poles and compared with the big pylons they seemed to have no truck with the race of time. One morning a hen appeared to have laid an egg, at least she exclaimed as hens do and then the dog barked and in a field not far distant workmen enjoined a beast to 'go on' to 'go on', and all the little topsides of all the olive trees swayed faintly silver, in the lovely sporadic breeze.

I was content there, content then. I could think of him or I could refuse to think of him. I was mistress of my thoughts and much more to the point, mistress of my heart. The only worry was when would the millionaire send for me and what kind of impression would I make on him. Two days had gone by and there was no summons from him. He had paid my fare and added a small amount for expenses. Madeline handed me the envelope with the new notes. I loved them, loved their pink and russet colour and the pictures showing a flight of steps that led to a square, and then the very patient, very resigned face of Michelangelo. Yes I was glad I had come.

I would stand at the one window for quite a long time and just stare at the forest that sloped down to a plantation of young vines, and then raise my eyes a fraction to follow the ground that rose about it, yellow ground, newly tilled. It is true that the cypresses unnerved me a bit. They spoke to me of ghostliness and perhaps they reminded me of death. I think now when I revisit that room that it was death they suggested but they were quite far away, on the horizon so to speak, while near me surrounding me were the little sturdy life-giving olives, the little nut trees and various other trees like nurselings and it was not death I thought of or dwelt on, but of Hart and myself slipping into bed, perhaps, one day or one night and snatching eagerly from life all the pleasure and all the satisfaction that might be ours. I would have liked him there and yet I did not want him there. I did not write to him, I did not even send a card. I flirted mildly with one of the other young boys and used to ask him to take walks with me so that we could identify the wild flowers. He was blond and blue-eyed, not as haunting as Hart, more acolyte than saint. One evening I had to take him to the hospital because his foot had swelled up after a wasp sting. While they drew the poison off it I waited in the corridor where there were scatterings of patients and visitors. At the end of the long room was a huge barred window and I walked down there and saw before me in true, magical storybook prettiness the street lights of Siena, the mountains beyond, and just above their peaks pathways of scarlet in the hushed blue vault of the heavens. Seen through bars, just like now. Here I get a mere fraction of sky and it could be grey woollen cloth, so opaque and unchanging is it. Yet as I stood there I did not mind the bars, in some ways they added interest. And I was not a patient. I thought that Hart and my son were probably building a stage at that very moment, giving orders, hammering, laughing, getting cables laid, working, clowning and I wondered why I did not miss them at all. The young boy hobbled towards me sporting a very big important bandage. I helped him out.

Thus in the twilight that was quickly passing we saw the façades change from beige and pink to a warm sultrier red, a red that seemed to exude life. The square was deserted save for a few cars and the houses like little palaces guarded the vast cathedral in the centre. It was one of those beguiling moments which causes one to say 'I could live here', or 'I will end my days here'; moments when it seems that the cares that bind us will soon pass, our shackles will turn into streamers, moments when even to ourselves we appear to walk on air, proud pirouettes impelled by the most propitious of gods.

We climbed the flight of steps that was dizzying in order to enter the cathedral and to light candles, perhaps to light candles for our separate intentions. But the iron-studded door was closed, and though we made some foolish attempt at knocking we were much more exhilarated by the thought of a grappa than the possibility of entering God's house. I personally did not care one way or the other. Sightseeing did not interest me. I had only one real desire, to get back to my room. The moment we got home I rushed up to see if anything had changed. But there was so little that could change. There was the big black wrought-iron double bed, with a mosaic in the centre of the bedhead. There was the chair that belonged more rightly in church, the wooden bench and a lampshade that was extremely incongruous being pretty and fringed. All in all it was a blissful combination. The lampshade and my variety of clothes that hung on the hallstand were what might be called the female elements in the room, while the other furnishings, gaunt as they were, fitted notably with the idea of male taste. A monk's room you might say, with a bit of floss. I had the conviction that I could stay there indefinitely, that those trees, and the way they swayed, or the way they unswayed, that the dog and the various other dogs whom I could hear but not see, that the hens, and the cypresses were my guardians, that by hiding there I could forget cities, forget insult, forget fear, even forget Jude, forget the hollowness of life. It is strange that though I loved the country and had daydreams about clay, about orchards, about things being planted, I lived in a city and saw things such as raspberries or lettuces in shops far removed from their source, as I believed I was.

I did not have to forget or banish Hart because in a sense I had not begun to cleave to the memory of him.

All we had had together was a dinner, a ramble up a street, and a surprise tea-time visit when he managed to convince me that he had left his sunglasses behind. We even knelt and groped for them although we both knew that it was one of those sweet ruses that bad liars, or intending lovers, resort to.

So in the mountain room with the rain outside, or if not rain, drizzle, I would open the windows and see the leaves blowing as it were in my direction, then lean out, smell the rain, hear the overflow in the gutter, hear the pit-a-pat on the leaves and occasionally the wind that was louder and more forceful. I thought, 'Stay here.' Was that a voice in me, warning, forewarning. But we have so many voices in us, how do we know which ones to obey.

The next morning I looked again to see if there was any signal from the millionaire. No letter had come. Madeline said he might put a flag out. He was the kind of man who did nothing in the expected manner, and for whom things had to be bizarre, even extreme. It seems he came to her villa one night in a carriage-and-pair, brought his own cook and a brace of pheasants. She even speculated on a little flirtation starting up between him and me but I doubted it. She said once I got in there I would be encompassed by the grandeur of it all. She said there was champagne in every room and no matter what the season white musk-smelling lilies. We could see his house behind the trees, it shone to advantage at night, was like a huge white ship, with lights twinkling on and off; at moments a sudden darkness, and then a fresh reinforcement of lights as if the life inside it was

83

passing through the most drastic, the most inconsistent of changes. She vouched he would send for me, but said that I must not wait on him and that if in fact I were out he would be all the more impressed.

We set off for a horse race known as the Palio. The town was in a fever of excitement. Although we had arrived early, every available seat was taken and still a crowds urged to get through. The town hall and the villas all around were festooned with flowers, flags hung from the various windows. Residents and their friends would lean out just to take stock of what was happening and presently withdraw. No doubt there were gatherings in most of the rooms, gatherings that had become a tradition from year to year. Very young boys in golden tunics with red epaulettes, and embroidered breast fronts, marched about, in a strut. Some juggled, some played the drums, others held the bright reins of the horses. The horses too were weighed down with bells, rosettes and other ornamentation. These horses were part of the pageantry, but the combatants, the ones who would race, were still in lorries at the back of the town hall, and sometimes in a lull one could hear them whinnying.

Eager for a good view we would try to edge our way into one place and then another and often we looked up with envy at those parties of people who merely had to lean out of their windows or loll on their balconies. The rousing music, the spontaneous outbursts from the crowd, the dazzle of the costumery and the cockiness of the boys added to the excitement. Rumour was rife at how dangerous the race could be, and death was not ruled out. We were told how horses and riders had often spilled their guts in the past and as if that were not enough how the losing jockeys would gang together to kill the winning jockey, with clubs. One of the boys who had learnt Italian was translator and if anything he seemed to understate. He was pale from the onslaught of stories told to him.

The more people who arrived the more frantic the throng became. The late arrivals would try climbing on other people's shoulders, or erecting their folding step-ladders. There was wildness about. Shortly before it began, the crowd lost patience and made it clear that they were no longer satisfied with music or spectacle, that they wanted the race. They began to stamp and howl. All heads were craned towards the big entrance door through which the horses came and then just as it was drawn back and the bugles sounded several of the women began to weep. At once as the horses came through, the roaring from the crowd became massive, and most people stood up so that to us who were at the back the event was something which we could only gauge from the shouting, the exclaiming, the booing and the wild contentiousness from rival groups. All we could see was one corner around which the horses came and while still craning to see we found our footing gone as a riderless horse broke loose and the crowd ran like wildfire, crushing each other in the process. It was as if a wall of swaying clamouring bodies all fell on one and I thought the day of general judgement had arrived, as we sloped towards the ground with bodies above, bodies around, and bodies beneath us. Yet almost as suddenly as we had been pitched, soon we were swung upright again like the wall that some master builder had miraculously restored. People were crying and screaming, some had fainted, several crossed themselves and thanked their maker. The horse was by now loose out on the street or else someone had managed to catch it. On the far side of the square the very same incident happened as we could discern from the pitiful cry of the people. When we stood up we saw people running in all directions, some to avoid catastrophe, others to seek it out. We ran ourselves not knowing what we wanted.

It was at least an hour before things quietened and not one of us knew who had been the winner, or what had happened to the winning jockey. The sand in the square still seemed to simmer from the impact of the hooves, and all around the place was littered with papers, ice-cream cartons and empty bottles. A restlessness had got into our bones. We bought and drank bottles of spirit. One of the young boys bought green bulbous balloons. Suddenly I found myself dashing to a souvenir shop to buy Hart a wooden flute. My party laughed as I tested it and caused unmusical sounds to issue out.

'Who is it for?'

'A boy,' I said.

Suddenly it was as if I had put my sights on him and as if from afar something had been set in motion. I must have known that I was going to see him, that I was going to couple with him and yet I would have postponed it for ever. There was a dance in the town square and we all trooped off. We danced with strangers, we drank anything that was offered to us. Somehow the flute got broken but I did not care. The strangers danced more robustly than I, but soon I was catching up with them and responding to their reckless embraces.

That night I had a dream that unnerved me. I dreamt I was with my lawful husband again, that we were man and wife, that I was scheming to leave him when he took me in his arms and said that we must never be parted from one another because we would miss one another dreadfully and I agreed. It was ghastly that agreeing of mine, because my uppermost wish was to leave him. I had always wanted to leave him but did not know how, because he kept watch over me and because he had threatened that if I did leave I would find myself committed to an asylum. But in the dream he was coaxing me and that was intolerable, because I knew that out of weakness, out of helplessness I might stay and to stay was death. I hated my lie, abhorred it, but knew no way, no trick, no speech, with which to undo it, unsay it, unbe it.

Yet the next morning what engrossed me was not my husband, not my employer, but Jude. I had that irrational longing to confront him with one question, one zealous question. When, at what precise moment did his heart harden and did his brain almost immediately say, 'I no longer love or cherish her, I believe I have begun to hate her.' Because hate he did. It is easy to read these signs, these imprimaturs. A coldness in the handshake, a kiss that merely passes for a kiss, but is in fact an insolent brush of the cheek. He began to talk of other women, of the wonderful egalitarian choice that any man, any would-be bachelor has in the city of London, all the more so in summer London, what with girls and women strewn in parks and gardens, and what also, with women as waitresses, barmaids, receptionists, masseuses, women zealous to serve.

'You must take me as you find me,' he would say, turning away to sleep. It is of no importance now and I wonder if the whole thing was not a bad hallucination.

WHERE will they send me? Some prison in the provinces where I will weave or cook or sew or learn patchwork. I will undoubtedly grow fat and listless or else I will grow thin. There seems to be no in between. I wonder if I could learn a lesson from those paintings that I saw in Florence. The very essence of them was their stillness, their inscrutability. They were faces that never disclosed what they had known, what they had seen, or what they had felt. They were like the faces of people who are the mere witnesses of their own predicament, who have gone outside it and are bearing it without a cry, or a whimper or a moan, even without a smile. I shudder when I think that I will never ramble with a colander into a kitchen garden again or search in the grass for the nuts – nuts, and ripe fruits – or hear the cuckoo or sit in a restaurant and savour those exquisite moments just before the others arrive, when the barman is slicing the lemons, and putting olives on a tray, with a little bunch of wooden skewers beside them. I will not lie in my own bath and hear the radio from the other room. I will not travel. I doubt that I will make love. Oh God I'm going to break down. I'm going to scream. I'm going to rail against God and man. I'm going to curse the womb that carried and later bore me, and the bottle that gave me suck.

The day after the Palio and feeling a bit cowed from my husband dream I decided to send a note to my employer to ask what he intended to do. The gardener took the note and set off on his little pop-pop bicycle. I had even groomed myself so as to be ready. The gardener was back in a short length of time with a note, but without my name on the envelope. I was a little daunted by the reply. The millionaire rebuked me for the way I had addressed him. He pointed out to me that when writing to a Duke one does not say 'Dear Sir' but that one says 'Dear Duke'. Madeline said it was a good sign, said he was taking an interest in me but now I dreaded my employment there. Yet in another sense I wanted to confront him, be a match for his innate contempt. That evening I set out for a walk in the direction of his estate. I thought I might bump into him. It was after sundown. I had been warned to avoid the deep grass because of vipers and so I went down a rocky little road, and up a rocky little hill, towards his grounds. I could hear tennis balls being hit in the distance, then clapping as if the onlookers were taking sides in a tournament. Perhaps he had a house party. There was an eerie absence of birds. Probably it is because they shoot them there. As I passed a small deserted-looking cottage, I stopped suddenly and went to the door and tried to push it in. Then unthinkingly, my eye just lighted on the spot where the key was, on the window sill under a stone. It was a very big key, big and unwieldy. For no reason I was opening this strange door when a workman went by and stopped. I thought perhaps he might accuse me but instead he put down his bundles of grass in which there were also bits of herb and wild flower, and helped me in my task. We went in together and looked at three sparsely furnished rooms, at a gas stove and at a lavatory. 'No luce,' he said pointing to the hole in the ceiling. Twisted bits of flex dangled from it. I had no idea why we went in and was very cheered to come out. He said something to me as he picked up his bundles and I followed and found myself in a hut, almost a cave, beneath the house. As he opened the half door and as we scrambled in I could hear a scurry in all directions. Soon I saw several coops and inside the wire meshing, rabbits with their ears pricked. He opened the lids of the coops and pushed the bundles of grass in, and as he did the rabbits became petrified and withdrew into the distantest corners. Their timidity disgusted me, the way they did not even grapple with their food, but obviously would wait until it was dark again so that they could nibble and chew, and then shit to their unilluminated, unspunky hearts' content. I even wondered if they would distinguish between the flavour of the grass and that of the flowers and that of the herbs. It was the epitome of depression and I wished that I had never seen it.

I took another road and there stomping towards me was the local lunatic – a man with a coat so tattered one would think it had been skilfully done with a shears. He had a soft hat pulled well down over his forehead and charcoal daubs on his face. I had seen his like a thousand times. I had only to re-see him to cringe again with terror and a sort of grudging pity for his existence, being shut up in a room, a loaf of bread on the table, a chamber pot under the bed, and drunkenness the day he got his assistance money. He muttered as he passed me by, then staggered on to the middle of the road and as soon as I decently could I began to run. Very soon a bell began to peal. There was a chapel in the grounds and I thought that in drunken venom it gave him pleasure to ring it to wrack our souls.

The sight of him, the pealing bell and the sudden memory of the painting of the little girl who had taken an apple from a stranger brought to mind all that I had felt about men in the long long ago. I thought of our juvenile dreams when we thought of nothing but weddings and trousseaux, when we thought we would be carried along on the prodigious pinion of man's valour. Us Gerties, us Nancies, us Dellas, us Kittys, us Kathleens, who believed that there was a species of gent quite different from the ones we knew, who would charge into town and carry us off. Many of us favoured or rather pre-favoured bank clerks, one thought of a chartered accountant without having an iota of what that meant, and I had a definite predilection for a dark and villainous gypsy with a kerchief around his neck, and metal teeth: one who would come in the thick of night on his horse and lead one away. What mularky. Novenas did bring a husband to one. To a Una. Us Gerties and Nancys and Kittys and Kathleens sat in Una's new drawing-room while she played with the cords of her new curtains, and while we admired the pelmet, then the smooth, the ever-so-smooth passage of the curtains as they met. The chief feature was the folds of material and the clusters of tumbling roses. Then one of the tittering girls had a brainwave or rather a non-brainwave because she suggested that the pattern, which is to say the roses, should face the street, be for the benefit and edification of the passers-by, and that the lined side should face the room. Una cogitated. Una was not pleased. We all volunteered an opinion. We were a hen party partaking of coffee and pastries. Una tapped her teeth. Una jumped up and telephoned her new husband at his office. Oh what blushes, what giggles, what innuendo once Una had got him on the line. Oh how we envied Una in her big new room, with its bowl of artificial flowers, with its two new unchipped decanters, its silver tray and its unused fireplace with a gaudy picture overhead. Una, on the phone, giggled. But how was it really. We ached to know. Did Una undress modestly on a landing, or did Greg, Una's husband, rip the garments from her. Did Una lie on in the mornings when Greg went off to the creamery where he was an assistant manager. Did Greg pet her thighs when he came in to lunch, did Una divest herself of her frilly apron, had Greg and Una quarrelled, did Greg move to the guest room in a huff one night because Una had asked for more housekeeping money. Did Una unaccountably cry in the afternoons and when she looked into the fire grate think how lonely early married days can be. Had Una yet begun to retch in the morning and feel nauseous, did she forget to water the plants? Did Greg complain as there was only one veg for lunch? Had Una gone to the local doctor, got on the couch, and gasped as he poked around and later said there was a little Gregory on the way. But of course as we sat with Una we gabbled about style and recipes and the fact that we still were hoping for you know who. Ah, the scullery-maid hotch-potch of hope. Soon a terrible tale unfolded. One of our hen party, Gertie, had been to a dance and had been asked up for a waltz by a long nosed gent. Long noses meant long fandangoes. Quite soon she realised that chit-chat was not to be the keynote of the occasion, since he tried to press through her, while making sure to keep her head and shoulders at a respectable distance. Only his lower parts were pressed towards her. Between gasps and giggles she was able to tell us that he had had the gall to position her pelvis and move his own hindquarters back and forth trying each time to get a fraction further into her. She did not say whether within the shemozzle there came a moment when she too went wet. She did not say. We gasped, commiserated with her and said how dreadful. Men the stampeders of our dreams.

I even think I should turn the tables. I should perhaps say that I am proud and jubilant to have killed one of the opposite sex, one of that breed to whom I owe nothing, but cruelty, deceit and the asp's death. Cite Dr Rat, renowned Dr Rat to whom I went for a cure. In my mind there was a doctor somewhere who would carry out an examination on me, make me say Aah, or even Ninety-Nine, see the dilemma and within minutes prescribe a miracle, a simple organic miracle. Except that he served poisons. I drank mine and swiftly felt the world turn into a spinning top. He assumed the properties of a rat. I could not hold him. Nor did he want to be held. Those hours, those bad hours brought the hair standing on my head, made the gooseflesh crawl while I was hurtled down, down, down, into the denisons of horror, with the devils to direct and make mock of my plight. The walls purred with blood, and the spheres through which I had to pass were lit by flame. There were no doors or no way out. Yet I had to get out, or die, or choke, and out I did get only to be dragged back again, back into the swirling sphere, and again and again with no respite, just the demons and the pits of blood and the horrifying despair. Above all, a helplessness, and one that I still feel when I remember that it seemed interminable and that one came out to the world only to be drawn back again, willy-nilly into the deep. Sweating and squealing. Dr Rat smiling a weird, Asiatic smile. Amused perhaps at the degree to which one human being, one simpleton, can become lost, damned, and consigned to bloodied eclipse. As helpless as spermatozoa. It was most valuable. I saw the rat people there, and knew that I would know them forever. The world that I came back to was indeed unswerving, almost exquisite. I was glad to feel the tableness of a table, to trot down a little path towards a garden seat and know that I would not be swept away. I used to concoct revenges for Dr Rat but I never carried them through. I saw him later at a soiree, watched his pale faraway face respond to a tune that was being played on the piano and I thought 'semi-murderer' but at any rate I was alive.

When he stood up it was plain to see that he was drunk and I knew that I had only to put my foot forward for him to trip and be the object of ridicule. Something stopped me but it was not charity. Cite him or cite Jude with his commercial traveller's kit of assorted romantic bilge. Yes indeed if I had killed wisely, that is to say judiciously, then Jude would be a gonner. Jude should be the one that I struck down and left for his aghast family to identify, to have an inquest on, to cremate or bury. I could have easily killed him in that hotel where we met for a weekend. Jude was there in his Scottish tweeds, Jude was shy but not so shy that when I climbed the wide staircase with its turkey carpet, and its brass rods that he did not follow, and when I walked into the big bedroom and thence into the big bathroom that he did not follow; and that when I opened a cupboard to see if there were enough hangers that he did not follow, and when in prank I stepped inside that he did not follow. He closed the door and there in a smother of dark, lust, love and cobweb we made love and swore never to be parted. Later Jude paced the bedroom and at times practised at a bit of imaginary golf.

Two days after the Palio I heard that the millionaire had taken off for Sardinia. But by lunchtime that information was contradicted. The little girl who did the laundry said she had seen him in his garden temple training one of his young hawks. I felt that I ought to announce my departure and yet I would postpone it, I would say 'I will do it tomorrow'. And so I lingered on. I bought Madeline little presents. I looked for signs to see if I was becoming unwelcome. I hid. As new guests arrived I dashed to my room in case they should be given it. An elderly lady in the room next to mine tossed and turned in her sleep, later snored. I put coats under the door dividing us to keep those sounds out. Everything began to exasperate me. The bites from the midges were intolerable, a wasp bite on my instep had swollen up, and I started to sleep for hours each afternoon, started to withdraw. One afternoon I dreamt of Hart, it was the first time I dreamt of him. He was with a nymph. She was not anyone I knew. Indeed she may be somebody nobody knew. She may not exist, she was tall and boyish, with blonde curly hair and of course she was naked. Her body was like glycerine, as wet and luminous as glycerine and it was as if she had just come out of a womb of sea. Hart sat at table with her, his head lowered and as on that first day with me an indescribable shyness possessed him, that and an indescribable loveliness. He could not do enough for her. He spoonfed her. Oh my grief. He was wearing a lovely brown velvet cling shirt, one that I believed I had given him. Had I seen it in a shop I would have bought it, regardless of cost. It had the colour and texture that one thinks of the earth as having, the real earth that is, that lies hidden under the earth we tread on.

Naturally my mother was there, my aunt was there, all these old faithfuls with their sorrows. We were all being dressed and made up for a performance. We were all going to play-act. My aged aunt wore a sailor's suit and a floppy sailor's collar and was a girl again. I tried but it was in vain. I could not make myself beautiful. My cheeks would not curve inwards though I daubed and daubed them with ochre stuff. He did not look in my direction. Why should he? I was insane with anger. He talked to her, laughed with her, then smiled at what she had said, then it was her turn to laugh, her turn to smile; and they even played little games that involved dice and thus the merest grazing of each other's fingers. Were they not in liaison. I thought this is how it will be, and when the play is over and when night falls and we all sit down to sup and we all disband, it is her stairs he will climb. He will desert me. She personified youth and liberty. I personified the clutch. I was of a mind within my dream to go straight across and slap her, deform her, brand her in some way. I even shouted that she had some sin, some flaw I could show him, some frailty but he would not look in my direction. Somehow I got myself up from the refectory table and went aside and gave myself a little tuition and said, 'This has been your fear, it is every-one's fear, this fear of being second, this fear of being dis-carded, this fear of being left and of being without.' And I strove within myself to take up arms against it, to pluck it out, to be done with it, indeed to be free.

And I thought I had succeeded. I remember how I still shook the next morning and how my breath was any-thing but rhythmic. I wondered what the others had dreamt. I wondered what they feared. There was a skin of milk on somebody's coffee because she had gone away to have a swim. When she came back I measured the size of her feet for fun by the imprint she made on the flagged floor. Pretty feet. The sun shone, the insects busied, amused and alighted themselves on every green leaf and every off-green leaf, on flowers and hairy stalks of flowers, on the warm air itself it seemed. Two people left so it was 'ciao-ciao' and kisses, and kisses and 'ciao-ciao'. A middle-aged man arrived, carrying only a rucksack. A taxi arrived with trunks. They belonged to the lady who snored. There were jokes as to who would carry them, but no one stirred. In the kitchen the servants chopped. The boy who had pimples, and talked a lot about suicide, lolled in the hammock. Coming across him, in any little nook or cranny, at sundown or sunset, he would leap forward, bow, excuse himself and ask you how much thought you had given to the subject of suicide. Now he was in the hammock kicking his legs up and down like a baby, while beside the swimming pool a woman put pearl nail polish on her toes and waited first for them to dry, and then for the pool to heat up. It was perfect. There was a cleanness in the air and the world seemed very propitious. My dream was beginning to rattle me less and I had begun to plan a day, a day composed of little events, walks, exercises, a few letters, wine.

Madeline looked at me sharply and called me aside. My heart gave a little swoon. I thought perhaps I had done something wrong, I had imbibed too much the night before, I had been snappy with one of the guests, I had used too much of the hot water, I had over-stayed. I thought of all these trivial things and began to quake.

We went up to her bedroom and she closed the door. One half of her bed was littered with books and papers, while the other half yielded a tossed white duvet. A round basket of jewellery with its tangle of gold chains and bright rings caught my eyes. A beautiful velvet-backed oval hand-mirror hung from a nail above the bed and resting against the opposite wall was a chest, with carvings of slaves on the lid. I thought what is it, what have I done wrong and I tried to be unperturbed, and she said, 'I have been thinking about this.' The very seconds ticked. She went on. 'I wonder, if perhaps we shouldn't winter here.'

I did not quite know what to say, considering the imaginings I had put into it. Nor did I know what she meant, not exactly. She was a lonely woman. She wore dark glasses in the morning. She had a kind of hidden flinch. Winter there? She was being ambiguous. Was I to be her lover, her servant, her companion, was it just us or was it the whole house party, and why? 'Winter,' I said, and thought instantly of how the valleys would be swallowed in mist, and realised that I had no idea what the olive trees would look like without their blustery silvery foliage. I thought of the days, and faithfully of the dark, a big fire at night, becoming secluded, grappling with one's habits.

'Just the two of us,' she said.

The thought of it did not repel me, but she must have felt my reserve because quite suddenly she put her hand to her hair, puffed it out and said, 'Only if it amused you.' But amusement would not be at the centre of it, I thought. There would be something else, there would be a time to be lived out, without props, and close to nature. She said to think about it, and then we linked and went down and gave ourselves a little cocktail as if we had just been through some sort of ordeal. I suppose we were, both of us, a little afraid, even shy. I walked to the village just to envisage what it would be like going there in the winter to collect my mail. Yes I would keep that link with the outer world. I sat and lounged in the cheerless hotel bar as the workmen drank and talked to each other, and glanced at the television which was blaring. I had bought myself a little dictionary.

There was a church opposite and behind it a stone tower. The people moved with infinite slowness. Occasionally the men glanced in my direction. I looked up the word for dark and then the word for smile. I expected that there was a doctor, a priest, a shoe maker, a bank manager, a dentist, and I supposed that in time we would get to know a few people and be invited to their houses and entertained rather stiffly in their stiff over-furnished salons. Not once did I think of Hart, not once did I pine for him, not once consider him. Yes once. I thought he might miss me but he would also be without the encumbrance of me. I thought how my son would not have the bother of me at Christmas and could spend it with a girl. I was receding. It was like going on a long voyage. Silly little matters occurred to me, like that I had a return ticket, which expired within a given number of days, that my bills would go unpaid, my garden would not be watered and that the cleaning woman in my house would assume that I had died. The night classes that I had signed on for, would have one missing person but that was nothing new. I was delighted at the prospect of Dee ringing, hearing the phone ring in the empty hall and eventually twigging to the fact that there was no one there. Jude might ring, late one night, buoyed with wine and the dregs of love. Or, he might write. I saw his handwriting, saw it there and then on a letter, his particular black spidery handwriting, that was like a thread, like pieces of thread inscribing my name on an envelope and I knew then how desperately I wanted to forget him. I would stay. It didn't seem like a foolish idea and I decided that I would sleep on it and tell Madeline the following morning when we had a moment alone. Also we would have to discuss money. I would have to do some work, any kind of work, in order to be paid.

Chance took up her loom again. Late that night I went out on my balcony to see the stars. They were at their most effective, a wonderful, a wizard pickle of stars in the deepest, densest, and most ageless of skies. The crickets sang perfectly as if conducted by a mastermind, the leaves rustled and I thought to myself how the nightly crop of mosquitoes were waiting to disport themselves on my flesh. A bell rang. The millionaire had got up and swung on his bell rope. It was of no importance. There was a smell of rosemary. All that was absent was the tinkle of sheep bells. I felt utterly at peace, utterly unharassed when all of a sudden there was a second bell as down below the phone had rung. In my nightgown without even waiting to get a shawl or a dressing gown, I ran and almost capsized as I took two and three steps at a time. I know now that I wanted it to be for me, that I knew it would be for me, and that despite all my vows I was waiting to get away. I was poised for flight. It was my son to ask how I was, and then to my amazement he asked if I would like to join them. Be, as he said, one of the troupe. I felt so young, so springing, so flattered. I felt my whole chest ring with excitement. It was like being someone who has been standing apart and is suddenly, mysteriously and without any warning drawn into a beautiful whirl. I said, 'Yes, yes.' Then he said, 'Can you hold on a minute?' Then Hart came on. His voice was tentativeness itself. He apologised for the faulty line. He asked how was my holiday. Then he said 'Have you said yes?', and I said, 'Yes, I've said yes', and I knew that when I put the receiver down I would be in possession of the most holy, the most hectic of happinesses. In the morning I was decked to go.

Madeline understood. She knew as well as I did, the call of a man, or of a boy, the mating call. She would stay on alone she reckoned, and raised her eyes as if to say, God only knows how. She is there now, helping perhaps to gather the grapes, or at least watching as they are pressed, through the big vats, and starting to ferment. She drove me to Florence, and we sat in a square as tourists do, sipping a drink, looking at other tourists and feeling sad at having to part. It began to pelt with rain and soon I hailed a taxi. The driver was a young boy and yes I have to say it, there was something enticing in his face, enticing and depraved. I had to do an errand for a friend in England, to collect two bronze pigeons which she had ordered. I showed him the address many times over. He would look at me in the car mirror and more than once I caught his eye. He had glittering blue eyes, blue as cobalt. It was pouring with rain. He asked if the friends were Italian and I said yes. I reckoned he was gauging whether he could overcharge me. The outskirts of the city had not the same beauty and not at all the same lustre. They were dun, modern, egg-carton concrete. I would hold up the piece of paper, with the address, and sometimes it seemed as if he understood, other times he looked puzzled. The meter was soaring. He turned it off. I asked why. He said we were outside the city boundary. It was going to cost me the earth.

Then in the blinding rain he got out to ask the way, then got back in, wiped his face with the hem of his T-shirt, and as he consulted his street map he leaned back and put his elbow above my knee near the crotch. There is no knowing whether it was three seconds, or thirty, but in those seconds I must have let him envisage high jinks.

He set off at a pleasant speed and without any pre-warning I saw that he had presented his penis. A penis like many another. Young, as he said, strong as he said, and packed with need. I decided not to. For a moment I could have, pandering to a random desire: and then again I could have, out of simple self-preservation except that I decided not to. I realised very clearly that this, this denial was my choice whereas his choice was his need to pursue it, even to the inevitable rape. Of course language divided us. I had a few words of Italian that I put to most industrious use. I resorted to the usual ploys, the usual protections, the usual words, such as that I was late, that I was menstruating and that I was married. He had no interest in such tosh. The rain was blinding, and now with only one hand on the wheel, and that, a very berserk hand, the tyres began to lose control. I envisaged an accident and thought spryly 'From the frying pan into the fire!' He suddenly swerved into a side road, over which grass grew, over which wilderness and emptiness presided. I knew for certain that there would be a scuffle within minutes. It was nearly dark. Strange to say I was able to notice the countryside, its particular ghostliness, the thick mist that lay over a hill of olives, the creepiness of the cypresses that after a rain seemed to draw a second cloak around themselves, a heavier blackness. The city itself was suspended in a kind of halo and I thought that down there were the paintings I had seen, the bright ones, the merry ones, the grave ones, the awesome ones staring out of their walls unseen, because the galleries would be shut. I could hear the car wheels sloshing over the potholes, and then all of a sudden he swerved into a thicket of trees, jumped out and was at my side while I still sallied on about terror, menstruation and marriage.

He was by my side. First thing I get is a bite on the shoulder and I am convinced that it is the poisonous tarantula. His tongue was rank. The hands careless at driving were binding me down and robbing me of my getaway. I had to make a choice whether to endure it and then have him drive me with my luggage, to the house, or else forgo my luggage. It galled me to lose favourite items of clothing, and more so the gifts that I had bought. He had almost submerged me. I realised that it was my mouth he wanted and somehow that was unbearable. I could not swallow his rank seed. I smiled, smacked my lips, gave him the impression that I would do all if I could just remove my jacket which was much too impeding. 'Caldo, caldo,' he said, agreeing. As he helped me out of it he let my hands come free. I pushed him from me with a deftness that I still applaud. I opened the door and sprawled out, feet first. For a second I thought my head was lopped, so forcefully had he grasped it. But I got it free.

'Cattivo, cattivo,' he shot at me and I knew it to mean bitch.

I was across the ditch and knew that he was following and it was a question of scaling a fence to get to the field beyond. He pulled at my leg and shoe. At that moment a lorry came round and by now standing on the wall with one shoe missing I flapped my arms desperately like a wounded bird. The lorry slowed down. The driver called to him. I jumped the wall and ran. I have no idea whether he followed me or whether he gave up the chase, but in the rain and through the swamp I must have covered two kilometres ending up without shoes and with legs scratched and skirt torn. The one thing I clutched was my handbag, the one means to eventual safety.

Oh, ornamental gates that guard a beautiful house, oh, stone house with arches, turrets, and long low loggias, will I ever forget you. The way you seemed to have an unrivalled story except that I could not learn from it, so silent were you, even your gates did not drip, even the turrets had no birds, even the windows no sundown in which an imaginary figure appeared. I came upon those gates and gripped them, so petrified was I from the run and what had preceded it. I think I shook them, but they did not move. Then I knew I had to walk on and so I did, half in dread and half in hope. Envisaging fresh catastrophe. It had become pitch dark and no sooner would I walk in one direction but I would decide that another direction was the right route. There was not a light from anywhere, and no sound of passing traffic. Where had I strayed to, and how much ground had I covered. I let out sounds and little consolations that were laughable in their meekness. Then having traipsed about uselessly, I resolved to go back to the big house and at least hide in one of the downstairs porches, until daylight.

Walking or rather groping my way towards there I decided to embark on a song, a jaunty piece, 'Waltzing Matilda'. It aided the motion. Then a miracle happened. A little figure came bending out of a hedge. It might have been part of the hedge so suddenly and so covertly did it appear. It said 'Buona Sera', and then 'Hello'. I told him my tale and at once he began to laugh, peals of laughter. Then he produced his flash lamp, and clicked it on and had a look at me. Next he handed it to me so that I might see him. He was holding a kitten in his arms and had it snuggled against his chest. He was a most beautiful little boy and even in the light from the flashlamp, I saw what smooth skin he had and what a cluster of lashes swooped from his lids. I followed him up the path, and then through a sort of plantation, and as we passed a hen coop he threw a stone in and shattered them in their slumbers. Then we climbed a stone wall and up another hill towards a house with a light in the downstairs room.

He let out a call and the door was opened. 'A man tried to kiss her,' he said to a woman, presumably his mother. So he had understood my story. He had even added to it. He said the man was drunk. He spoke to her in Italian and translated for me, into English. He was very proud of his mission. The woman was frowning and I felt she didn't believe me. I must have looked more like some-one who had escaped from an asylum. With folded hands and some sort of genuflection I begged her to let me in. He threw the kitten down and said something to her in Italian and then I knew I was being admitted.

It was a night of indescribable beauty and happiness, a night perhaps such as is sent to people before or after an ordeal. She gave me something to eat but I do not remember what or if I touched it. She gave me antiseptic to put on my wounds and I heard myself say that I would like music. I pointed to their record player and within minutes there were the various sounds of Africa, and between those sounds beautiful trickles of music. The sounds were of animals, of storms, of danger and of menace. As if by contrivance it began to thunder outside, huge visceral claps of it, rumbling the house. The little boy was jubilant. He ran to the window and parted the curtains just at a moment when a jagged sheet of light-ning was tearing the sky. Then he closed the curtains and would part them at just the right moment to catch the next fork. After a while he sat next to his mother while a little girl, presumably his sister, sat on the other side. At moments he and his sister would bicker, or pinch and immediately the mother would deliver a biff and then be accused by both for having biffed the wrong person. The yellow light bulb had splashes of gold leaf on it and there were fresh tea roses on a jug; these summoning up

England and the small patches of garden that tumble
down to the edge of the railway line so that all at once
passengers see hollyhocks and lettuces and gilded
trellises over which dog roses, wild roses and every other
kind hang like lanterns. On the wall there was a photograph that at first seemed to be a waterfall, but in fact
it was of a nude woman reclining between cliffs. The
cliffs were dark and shaggy, whereas she was snow-
white. The little boy said that she had two boobs and a
bush in the middle. He was quite amorous. The music
and the thunder got to our bodies and yet everything in
that room was the essence of stillness. It was so still that I
even noticed when the little boy furtively turned the rug
over, to show that it could be used on both sides. It was
one of the three times in life that I wanted never to end.
The second was when Hart made a proposal to me, and
the third was on the day of my first Holy Communion
when the host seemed to fill the inside of my body with
all the ecstasy I had ever craved, and the white satin dress
and fine veil were a gauze between me and the world.

When they did fall asleep the young patient mother
picked them up, one on either side. I could not bear to
see them go. Only the slippers that had fallen from their
feet remained, like toys, and out of some maternal instinct I put them neatly in front of the fireplace, the very
same as if the fire were lit and I was warming them.

I stayed the night, but did not bother with sleep. I sat
upright on the sofa. There was a huge brown pod full of
seed and I held it and rattled it hoping that the little boy
would come back. He did come, much much later, when
it was nearly dawn and sat on the arm-rest of the sofa
while I sat at the other end and watched him. He pointed
to his toy jungle, then blackened his face with crayons

and presently said, 'I steal, but I won't steal from you.'
I would have liked to know why he spoke one language
and they another, or what he was doing out in the fields
at night, or why he was such a little master, or why his
mother was so quiet almost to the point of being mute.
But I couldn't. The event accidental in itself was so
strange, so spellbinding, that I did not want to tamper
with it, nor learn anything about their everyday lives
which no doubt resemble most other everyday lives. I
reckon for them too the night was not without essence
and I am certain that I did not dream them.

That morning in the city I had a spree, perhaps my last
spree. I dined in a restaurant where everything was
ordained – a delicious smell, pale-pink tablecloths with
napkins that matched, small bowls of fresh dampened
flowers, as many waiters as customers so that one could
chat about the weather, the tourists, and the gouaches on
the walls. Perfection. A napkin folded around the handle
of a teapot exactly where one's hand would be likely to
grasp it. It is odd that at times life is so utterly stream-
lined and then all of a sudden a battleground. Somebody had left a paperback book on my table and its
blurb said that the only grass Alfred Hitchcock got high
on was the kind that grows in the cemetery; and the
only acid that blows his mind was the sort that could be
thrown in someone's face. It seemed so forced and so
ridiculous. I had bought new shoes and would stoop
down to admire them and to feel the softness, the glove-
like-ness of the fawn kid. They were pointed toes and
I have a feeling that they are about to be in fashion.
Again as I sat there a sort of miraculous leisureliness

took charge of me and I had to force myself to get up and go. Weeks after when I was in Scotland and saw the birds preparing to migrate, I wondered if at least one of them wanted to tag behind or is nature flawless in that way.

At the airport we had a very long wait. The vendor who sold hamburgers did a fantastic business and hardly bothered to toast the scones he was serving them between. They were tasteless. The same people kept traipsing up and down and shortly I knew many of the faces and even wondered about them. It was easier to wonder while they remained silent. Their voices, or rather the thoughts that these voices amplified, were less fascinating than the mouths or the eyelids or the expressions that speak of untold things.

Dark brown scutter was all over the several lavatory seats and the bowls had been stuffed with newspaper. As the holiday was nearing its end I longed with a considerable ache for my own house, my routine, my books, telephone calls, my son, and Hart's eventual smile when I next shook hands with him.

The Scottish sky was darker, broodier, all those sloping hills and crags housed the spectres of battles and the drones of witches or that is how it seems now. Anyhow the light was different. We perhaps never see what we are seeing, and never cease to try to re-see until our brains are bursting with a variety of impressions about a thing that is no longer possible to confront. The sheep were like ethereal flocks scattered on slope and valley, and they scarcely moved. It had not rained in an age. The grass was dry, the gorse was tawny, the moss on the stones a bright furry thirsty green. Soon I would see him.

Except that I didn't. No welcome awaited me, as they were all busy and work had consumed them. Think of it, they did not even excuse themselves from rehearsing to welcome me in. A strange boy called Bates showed me to my room. He sucked so considerably on his finger that I wished I had brought a baby's bottle. Then the room, another disappointment. It was a little room on the ground floor that looked out on to a stone courtyard and had no access to the sky or the surrounding woods. I thought how radically climate changes the spirits and already mine lagged.

It was Bates's house and the troupe had the use of the stables and a few of the downstairs rooms. I threw my case on the iron bed and thought in that sour way that one does, what I was doing to have surrendered a holiday, beautiful surroundings, miraculous paintings, pleasant friends to hie myself to a place where not a scrap of cheer awaited one. Already I had seen the kitchen, having gone in for a glass of water, and it was cheerless and dark. Nothing but cereal packets, large sliced loaves and the breakfast plates with the grease congealing on them. Bates rushed back to rehearsals leaving me to consider my lot.

A nondescript room not quite a guest room and not a maid's room, a sort of box room with one picture on the wall – a brown reproduction of a toiling couple in the field who have stopped to say the Angelus. There was also an old calendar from a boot polish manufacturer. It had a movable rectangle to mark each day but this too had stuck. Nets of cobwebs hung from the corners and the shutters did not fasten. I thought that no doubt there would be the inevitable boring yet unsettling story about a ghost and I already envisaged one as living wretchedly in a cavity in the stone column that supported the twisted stairway. I had brought from Italy a punnet of figs to present to him so that he could have a taste of the landscape, but now in my cussed mood I began to eat them alone. What is more I donned a dark sombre dress. Brightness had gone from me and those beautiful open squares where I lolled, sipped coffee and watched the passing parade, these were figments indeed, figments suspended in tinted light.

They were in the music room rehearsing and when I tiptoed into the gallery my son was scolding them. I wanted to run away but as always embarrassment glued me to the spot. He almost screeched as he strode about and he was stooped because of wearing several layers of ridiculous ladies' cardigans. He was of course making a tremendous effort to be their senior, the one who told them what to do. One of the girls, Wynne, was making a rabbit out of her spotted handkerchief and he asked her in God's name to cut it out but she shrugged.

The place was freezing and the acoustics were bad. Then I saw Hart and I felt everything in me quicken, like the aspen rod. I think he caught my eye but he gave no signal and he did not wave. A black satin scarf was loosely knotted about his throat and his face was radiant. Perhaps he was flushed because of the row in progress.

Once again they began to rehearse and it seemed to me that they did put a little more command into it so that the lines struck one as having some potency. I felt waves of loneliness and chided myself for having surrendered a cheerful villa and my beautiful room, my nest, to come and sit in a cheerless draughty gallery in order to hear impassioned words about death delivered mechanically. But there I was.

We lunched out of doors under an oak tree. The lunch consisted of thick slices of home-made soda bread, covered over with a pink meat paste. There was a bottle of barley water passed around and I thought with longing of the warm pool where I could be now sitting, enjoying the first glass of wine, and having perhaps an anchovy on a thin triangle of toast. I told them a bit about Tuscany, its memorable landscape, meals I'd eaten, chapels I'd seen, and then, rather clumsily I produced a thick pack of postcards. But they were discussing what there ought to be for dinner, and whose turn it was to prepare, so that my conversation seemed luxuriousness indeed. Hart did look at the cards and then holding up a postcard of the Annunciation he asked if I had seen it. I hadn't. He smiled, gleeful, then tapped his chest to say that he had and I was not sure but that he was competing. For no reason I asked him his favourite colour and he said he would rather not say. Wynne put a loose coil from the brass bottle top, the one from the barley water, on his ear lobe and at once he looked like a villainous gypsy.

It was a sultry day and the picnic spot under the oak tree was crawling with midges. They began to light on my existing bites so that I imagined a pyramid of bites contracted in different places, at different moments, all accruing to make me blotched and itching for life. I feared that soon I would be tearing at my flesh through my clothes and my stockings and to avert it I dug my nails and fingertips into the cracked dry earth. One of the actors was having his lines heard so that conversation was ruled out. There was a sullenness about them all. I could see the girls eyeing me, looking at my clothes, the beautiful pointed new shoes, the handbag, sizing them up. One of them was blonde and very pretty and I wondered who she had paired with and thought she's probably with Hart. I began to scratch the bites, giving a thorough rasping vindictive scratch to each one, so much so that Hart asked if I was allergic. I felt he was making fun of me and at once I stood up and demanded from my son that he accompany me on a walk. He was so distracted that at first he walked into a yew tree and this brought bumble bees out and led to a considerable mass of droning.

'How is it going?' I said.

'V. bad,' he said, not realising that I wanted to talk about something else. He went on about their little catastrophes, how one of the girls had to be sent home with jaundice, how another of the boys was trying to jilt Rebecca and how Wynne tended to burst into tears on stage, particularly at the moments that were supposed to be funny. Rebecca it seems was the pretty girl with the bleached hair and the black velvet choker. I said how off-hand they all were and he said that was to be expected, considering their problems. No one had learned their lines, they were opening in Edinburgh in three days, and they would be a laughing stock to the public as well as a liability to the university who had sponsored them.

'I never saw my millionaire,' I said, and added that probably I would not get paid. Another obstacle. At that moment I wanted our worries, our funds, to be understood; I was even on the point of continuing that endless saga as to whether or not we should leave our house and move to a cheaper one.

'It's not our summer,' he said. He was wizened from cares and I felt that he had wearied of his new girl friend. She had sat like a statue through lunch, not eating, staring at him, and absently crumbing the bread that was in the basket.

'It is,' I said and then I linked him and gave him the hug that I'd been hoarding for him ever since I arrived.

'How is Hart?' I said, whispering.

'Hart is the best of the bunch,' he said, but that was not what I had wanted to hear.

That night someone lit a fire in the music room and we ate supper off our laps. I had walked to the town and hauled back bottles of wine and I was thanked by one and all as they quaffed it. One of the girls sat at the piano and idly fingered out a few tunes. I asked my son if he might sing and after an amount of coaxing and various demurs he started. He closed his eyes as he always does, the better to concentrate, the better to assume the emotions of the blind Irish harper whose sad tale he was telling. One of the girls, Eileen, sang a suggestive song about Sir Jasper and a maid who got between his lilywhite sheets. The maid said no-no-no until such time as she capitulated and said yes-yes-yes. I kept watching Hart's face and it was surprising that no expression leaked through, save for the fact that he enjoyed the surroundings, that he asked permission before taking anything to eat and that he drank sparingly of the wine. He mixed it with water and in deference I began to do the same, but he didn't notice. Presently it was his turn. He and Bates had a duet that they had learnt when they were at the same boarding school. It was a shanty song and each line described a different incident at sea. We were all asked to join in the chorus, the 'hey-ho hey-ho' type of thing.

Bates stole the limelight. He sang the first five lines and then reluctantly allowed Hart to sing the sixth. Instead of bridling or cancelling his smile Hart accepted it and let the song jog on, joining in the chanting only. I was so struck by his reserve that there and then I wanted to give him a beautiful present. I thought of a gigantic sweater in brown bouclé with each knob of wool like a burr that had stuck on. I tried to catch his eye but he shunned me. Yet I felt for certain that he knew that my gaze was upon him. Possibly he decided that by acknowledging it he was slighting all the others. The girls did fancy him and Wynne doted on him. She would drink from his glass by mistake, or borrow his knife, and at one point she gobbled a piece of cheese that he had just brought to his exquisite parted lips. The action made me spring to my feet in order to prevent it. I felt violent. Of course once up I had to dance in order to give some credence for my action in standing so suddenly. It was laughable. I dangled my arms and did a sort of dance that succeeded in making everyone laugh. No, we would not be lovers. My homeward dash had not been precipitate, it had been in vain. I reckoned that the night he and my son rang was one of those enchanted nights when two young men buy a half bottle of whiskey, sit down on a step, discuss their futures and all in all paint a glorious untarnished picture for themselves. We would not love. To have even entertained such a thought was reckless, was puke, and the pathos, the shit pathos and the subsequent dependence of it all already sickened me, even though now it was not about to happen. I could easily foresee the million ways in which I might wrestle for his attention – a look, a smile, a graze of fingers, a touch, my name spoken – how zealously I would search for these, and more and still more, until like a glutton I would stop at nothing. Whereas now I saw I was free.

I excused myself around midnight and skedaddled off to bed. However the events of the day proved too much and I could not even attempt to sleep. The faces from the airport and now the various faces of the troupe appeared before me, but in different stages of distortion. I saw a lot of lips, just lips suspended in the atmosphere, moving and pursing, many with moustaches. The airport announcements got muddled up with the lines of the play and many of the troupe were in mediaeval costume. Hart was poised on a hound made of stone and he was smiling as he embarked on a crusade. I thought how like Michelangelo's David he was and I did not know that I would think that again but in the direst of circumstances.

My room was hot and stifling, also it adjoined the bathroom, so when it wasn't one of them trundling in there, it was the chain being pulled, or it was water in the tank letting out the most ominous, the most disruptive of sounds. Just as well, I thought, not to be entering the mad bazaar of love again. Unbearable to watch it move and unbearable to watch it remain static because that would mean death. Unbearable to watch the slow, the vicious, the frosty, the fingering inculcations of life, the day-to-day crush, to watch it die.

In the morning I asked Bates, privately, if I could change. He put me in another wing of the house but the room was of the same ilk. I left my belongings in the first room as we were due to leave the next morning. It

117

was a frantic day and everyone kept bumping into one another and not even uttering a cursory sorry or excuse me. I heard a sample of Hart's acting as I passed through the music room and thought it very unsure. Tiddy, the quiet girl, and I were given the task of dyeing clothes and making metal shields. We had to beat out bottle tops with hammers and every time I hit my fingers Tiddy said 'Crumbs!' We took time off unknownst to them and gathered gooseberries to make a pie. She snagged them, while I made the pastry and when we each carried one aloft into the music room at tea-time, they were as jubilant as if we'd brought the fatted calf.

We had to retire very early as we were leaving for the city at seven, because they had a dress rehearsal. People went to bed in dribs and drabs. I went before Hart did. He stood up as I took my leave and even wondered if I'd forgotten a bag or a shawl, searched as I myself might have done.

I did not like my new room as the bed was too narrow and the walls had the wrong smell. They smelt like a lime kiln. I was rubbing my midge bites and dreading a second night of agitation when all of a sudden I heard a door bang then footsteps and thought 'Ghost'. I expected that some kind of figure was going to seep through the lime-smelling walls. I watched in the dark with every perception on edge, waiting to see who would enter and by what means. It even occurred to me that some of the troupe might be playing a trick on me, and might come in wearing masks. The waiting got too much, or rather the waiting without the climax, so all of a sudden I got out of bed, left my room, crossed the stone corridor, went down a stairs, went a bit astray, climbed another stairs, crossed another cold corridor and returned to my old room. The land I got! There he was sitting on my bed with a tube of ointment in his hand. I said nothing. He may even have assumed that I was with another. I just crossed to him and put my wrists out so that he could put the ointment on the bites. Then I offered my legs, offered my chest, and then at last I looked at him and there was the most smiling, the most uncritical, the most lovely beaming face, and without even thinking what I was doing I clicked off the light and nestled near to him. He held me. I held him. That was sufficient. He had a little torch, one he used because of sleeping in the granary. He lit it and left it on a bedside table. Still in an embrace we removed pieces of one another's clothing and crept into bed. It may be that some people fit more snugly together, and need no preamble, no introduction to one another's bodies. There we were, lying perfectly still and talking cheerfully. It was not like love-making, it was almost passionless, almost with a breath of sanctity.

'Will I get the blame if you're not on form tomorrow,' I said.

'You will,' he said.

'But who was here waiting,' I said, a little crushed at his lack of ardour.

'I thought your bites needed me,' he said, and felt their little mounds and made jokes about them.

I told him about Italy, the walks I'd taken, the day the chapel bell pealed out, my last day, the would-be rape.

'An adventuress,' he said.

I had to squeeze conversation out of him. He said that once he had worn a golden earring and with my finger I searched for the little hole but it had closed up. He had been very ill once, and was put in a glass unit, under supervision, and they had removed his earring lest he cut himself with it. I did not ask what kind of illness; I assumed. But when he described being in the glass cage I saw the years slip off him, I saw him as a little child, in some sort of playpen, hopping about. It was uncanny the way he described things without any excess. I thought that if I were young again I would cultivate simplicity. It was the same with his clothing, a long linen shirt, a black scarf, jeans and a pair of sensible mountaineer's boots.

'Do you cry much?' I said.

'Yeh. . . at the cinema,' he said, and warned what a very bad escort he would be.

'And what do you want to be?' I asked.

'A bum,' he said and hugged me, apologetically.

Yet in the autumn he was going on to another university to take a post-graduate course. His father had given him a cottage, and he was looking for someone to share. He described the kitchen, its old grey stove, a pantry, a meat safe, and then two rooms with boards that creaked. He said it was a bit depressing and I said that he could paint it, paint it siena red. He laughed and said I was siena mad. But those colours I saw in those squares at dusk did seem the most perfect and enriching colours, a feast for mind and eye. I would like all rooms, especially my future abode, to have that colour, to give off a glow.

Having talked so much we realised that we were starving and he crept off to the kitchen to pillage. I was smiling to myself while he was away, smiling at how inevitably it had happened. He came back with two ripe bananas and the remains of a ginger cake in a doily. It was while eating we began to make love. A sort of childish devilment had got into him as he was gobbling up the last bit of cake, then he licked the doily, then suddenly put a few remaining crumbs in my mouth. It was as if he were the senior one, so calm was he, and so assured. I did not resist or say anything about the inadvisability of it. As with the elements the unforeseen happened. A few moments more, a batch of kisses, the right embraces and he had carried roses to my limbs. We might have been bedded down on silk sheets, we might have been at sea, or in a gale-force wind, so wild, so stormy, and so rapacious was the time that followed, and his mouth and all the rest of him were like lava spilling over me, unending and tireless.

I knew it would be followed by an awkward shyness and indeed it was.

'There is no need to go on with this,' I said.

'As you wish,' he said, and he sealed it with a dry kiss.

Afterwards it was impossible to sleep. For one thing it was almost morning and as he said to doze would be most unwise since we soon had to get up. He pulled the sleeping bag up to our chins and in doing so left our toes to the cold.

'Will they know?' I said.

'No,' he said. He said it with an assurance that astounded me.

Did he leave his bed each night, was he a philanderer, had he slept with all the others? I put my cold feet over his and he let out the most boisterous of sounds. Certainly his whereabouts was no secret to anyone passing by.

Of course downstairs and in the company of the others we were at a loss and I could not look at him. He boiled an egg and offered it to me. I was almost curt. I said I hated boiled eggs. The clothes Tiddy and I had dyed were on hangers in the kitchen and made an incongruous and startling sight. Mauve kaftans with motifs and floppy caps with gold braiding gave the place an odd glamour and were suggestions of carnival. Wynne was writing her name with a knife on the kitchen table. She then wrote his name and there they are, side by side, crudely hacked out on a white bleached ash table. It is nearer to him than I am, at least in the eyes of the world. I have a longing to be connected with him still, to have our names next to each other on some register, even on a graveyard slab. You see I believe I did love him and that there was kernel to it and that I love him now but how shall I go on bearing it. Ah, who cares about infinitesimal things.

When we set out in the lorry I was asked out of deference to sit in the front next to the driver, and to my chagrin, Bates got in next to me. They were sorry to leave the place and let out all sorts of exclamations. I was pleased. Already it had begun to look grey and lonely and I thought how the winds would whip around it in winter and how maybe Hart or I would go back in memory and explore the bedroom with the lime-kiln smell. I was glad of our cavort but I knew that I must not cling to him, must not. They dropped me at my hotel. A shabby little dump with a misleadingly beguiling soft red light outside the hall door. Their stage manager had booked it for me. They were all going to Wynne's house but I had not been invited. I felt bereft as I wished them luck and planned to meet my son after the dress rehearsal. I saw Hart look at me, flinch, as if he wanted to jump out of the lorry and say something to me, something as I imagined, polite and conclusive and gentlemanly.

THE HOTEL BEDROOM was unenticing, what with its pokiness, cracked washbasin, stained handwoven bedspread and an appallingly garish plastic lampshade. I thought that if he visited me on any pretext we would be wretched, and completely abashed. I opened the locker, took out a grey blanket, hugged it out of necessity. Then resolving to make the best of things I opened the suitcase, got out the photo of my son, got out my clothes, hung them, got my bottle of perfume and sprinkled myself recklessly with it. I was just reading a drinks menu pinned to the wall and debating whether to have wine or whiskey when there was a knock on my door.

'You're wanted,' a girl said. She made no effort to elaborate, to say by whom or why. She was a strapping girl. I followed and just caught up with her as she was on the point of closing the folding door of the tiny shuddery lift.

'By whom?' I asked, getting in beside her.

'Phone,' she said. She was subversiveness itself. I expect I knew.

'Guess what.' It was Hart's voice at the other end, buoyant with excitement.

'The play is cancelled?' I said.

'We're just across the road from you.' It was like resurrection.

'This is a dungeon,' I said, not caring if she heard.

'No dining-room,' I said. 'No tea, no toast.'

'I'll give you tea,' he said.

We met in the street as he came across to fetch me and we were so overcome it was as if we had parted weeks before. I knew then that there was a bond. The others had gone to the theatre but he was excused because of having a big part and a bit of a sore throat.

'Liar,' I said, and he almost bore me up the steps and into the big oak-panelled hallway, and thence to his bedroom where we could be private.

My last opportunity to turn back, to say no, to stand alone as I had always vowed to. Instead I stood by the window, muddled, devoid of resolution. A mossy slate roof jutted out beneath. The moss was wet, the slates a shining pitch black varnished almost, and over these slates the pigeons and the littler birds trotted and none of them ever once lost their footing. They pecked incessantly. He had come behind me but he had not touched me.

'What are they pecking at?' he said.

'I have no idea,' I said.

I was shaking. Happiness, indecision, the thrust of the leap because is it not always a leap, that journey over to another, to any other, once one decided to make it.

'Why are you shaking?' he asked.

'Because I do,' I said.

But the real reason was my thoughts and my predicament. Without him I would have been alone in that hotel bedroom totting up the old needs. I knew how stupid that situation was, in fact it was stupidity incarnate. It was the very same as if the emotional flesh was grated and grated and grated until it came away in bloodied maggoty bits. Any fool knows that when you have grated flesh to its utmost there is only one place you can reach and that is bone. Perhaps that is why I shook. Or else I wanted to be rid of him. Well I am now.

'You said we would not go on with this,' I reminded him.

'Just while I do the play,' he said.

'Why?' I asked.

'Because it's glorious,' he said. Such a silly and inappropriate word. I could not resist it. He took me in his arms and held me until the noise of the whistling kettle sent him dashing to the kitchen to make tea.

Although he was in the room only a matter of minutes it was already his. He had tumbled things out of his rucksack and for some reason I was immensely moved by the sight of his dressing gown laid across the bed. It was a paisley dressing gown and there was something very sedate about it. When he came back he said he would rather that I did not see the play until they improved, also that I might make him forget his lines. I took a little ebony mascot from my bag and gave it to him for luck. He kissed it. He was like that. He cannot know how happy he made me.

'There is the joyful, the sorrowful and the glorious,' I said, recalling the mysteries of the rosary and perhaps because of this childish moment between us I felt a longing to be restored to the order and litany of my youth.

'It won't be sorrowful,' he said. He was as grave, as old and as time-worn as a pumice stone.

Yet he was quite different when they got home from the theatre in the evening. They were all completely

125

engrossed in each other, in what happened. They ate while still talking and walking around. The soup that had taken hours of peeling, simmering, sieving, thickening, flavouring, was downed in seconds. My son winked at me and said 'Hiya'. They might have been drunk so scatty were they as they each told each other how exceptional everything had been. Apparently it went well. When he gave Wynne his cap to wear I felt myself bridle. I expect she asked for it when she whispered in his ear. She wore it at an angle, very jaunty. Then she tried other ways of wearing it, then she got a measuring tape so that she could compare the size of their heads. So there they were, laughing and joking and there was I, edging away from him. Except that he hardly saw me. Like most of the others he had left his make-up on, and his painted face was ravishing. He had a line of kohl under the eyes and his pupils seemed big, and mad and dancing.

Many lives and destinies suggested themselves in that painted countenance and I saw him as one driving a sleigh, one in pursuit of strange and difficult and beautiful things. At other times he was but a boy eating his cereal, always aloof and weary almost. But both times either as boy or lover I wished that he was an image, someone to whom I could pray, someone without carnal love and carnal punishment.

I announced to them that I would like to light a fire. It became something of momentous importance to me. I held a double sheet of newspaper in front of the grate and he came across to help me. He saw my pique. He said he would tell me later, he would explain later. Already I disliked my terms. We were both eager that the fire should catch, and visibly disappointed each time when as we removed the sheet of paper a pile of sullen black coal met our eyes. He went off and got a wooden box, then laid it on the red tiled kerb, and knelt on it and soon we had a supply of kindling. For some reason I was reminded of an evening when I sat on a wooden box under an elder tree and a drop of the juice had dripped on to me. The others gradually went off to bed. Except for Wynne who hovered. Then she too left. Then he took both my hands and said that there were three reasons for his silence. The first that he could not think of anything sensible to say to me in public. Second that he was a bit of a bastard. Third that he felt Wynne might feel left out. She crept back to the room and saw our held hands. He did not turn round to welcome her back. She saw this and stood and gave a most flagrant glare. Then she threw his cap into a far corner and went out.

'Will you stay with me?' he said.

'She'll know,' I said.

'Let her know,' he said. I was delighted by his first show of courage.

In the morning Wynne brought his tea. Her eyelids were pink. God only knows what hurt and hatreds she had conceived. She placed the mug of tea between our bare shoulders.

'No tea for me?' I said, trying to be bluff.

'Get it yourself,' she said. When she went out I asked if he was afraid of her and he said, 'Slightly.'

'Women,' he said and he gave a little shudder. For the first time I saw the thin raised thatch of black hairs on the rim of his shoulder and I felt repelled, almost afraid.

'I'm a wolf,' he said, and not for the first time I

realised how marginal an earthly love can be, how the littlest change can make us defect, can make us flee.

At breakfast Wynne and her best friend communicated with sign language. It was about us, about our soppiness, and how we ate snacks in our room. The paper he was reading was snatched from him, so was the sausage that he intended to put in his mouth. He smiled at me on and off. I see those smiles now as miraculous torches that were clicked on, and that I in my madness succeeded in extinguishing.

Later I went back to my hotel to have a bath and a sleep. I was resolved that we would not see too much of one another. I did not want to trail him. Anyhow the years alone had made it necessary for me to withdraw in order not to be seen to be in an unbecoming spin.

So on the Sunday morning while they were still busy in the kitchen, I put on my coat and said that I was going to sightsee. To make extra money they had decided to serve tea and chocolate gâteau in the afternoons, in the foyer of the theatre. He consulted me about its consistency, did it need more chocolate, did it need vanilla, was it too runny, what temperature should the oven be at. There was such a hilarity about their cooking, such a palpable lack of anxiety, such a ravenous mirth as they tasted raw dough and went yum yum, that I wondered if I had ever been young at all.

I sat on a bench in the town gardens and listened to the band play. Not far away, on a box, a fanatic was exhorting mankind to listen to God. The leaves were being blown and a few had already turned.

There was a crowd of youngsters around the ice-cream van and though I tried to put him out of my mind I could not. Looking at the town clock I knew that by now he and the others would have gone to the theatre, to serve the tea and slices of warm cake. I was saying that it was courting disaster to get myself entangled, and yet vouching to go on with it, to make such an impression that I would come between him and his former self, come between him and all others. I looked up to consult the town clock and it was as if I felt the smile the way one feels the first drops of rain.

'You got lost,' he said.

Oh what a smile! He even had his glasses on, and judging by his flush he had been running around from one venue to another, in search of me. Just then the trumpet was playing. I stood up and kissed him. Loving his mouth as I did, I was under the mistaken impression that my own would take on the exact imprint and shape of his, and that my upper lip would curl up becomingly. We walked, not knowing where to go. We walked so close, and so joined together that we must have seemed like two deformed people, bundled. I remember seeing couples, and families, and solitary strollers, but only as one sees them in some inner zone, as one might see lilies or vegetation in the bottom of a pond. It was probably what is called 'being out of this world'.

We crossed the road and glided towards a big hotel, went through the swing doors still bundled together. The lobby was vast and though it was daytime the lights were on. They were bright bulbs suspended from curling brass branches. In the other room a vista of cream and coconut cakes on a trolley and the sound of a pianist playing 'Autumn Leaves'. On the way through we stopped to read a notice that carried the Selkirk Grace –

> Some hae meat, and canna eat,
> And some would eat that want it;
> But we hae meat and we can eat,
> And sae the Lord be thankit.

He said he wanted to fly. Being young he could say these things and I could support them. The previous girl had not encouraged him to fly. Not that he maligned her. He simply said that he had been too young. Was my age being shared with his. Might we, as I ruefully, secretly, thought, put our two ages into a little box, shake them up then halve the years. The years I saw as golden digits. My aura he said was cream. I seemed not to relish that, but he stressed how glorious cream was. Thick cream with strawberries. I suppose he thought of night and how he used to eat me, in a manner of speaking. He said so little. I was beginning to say less.

THE NEXT DAYS are a blur. Like a stroll in the sun – warm and drifting with no destination in mind. Mostly we were silly, daft. Wynne found a note I'd left on his pillow and brandished it in front of all the others.

Even the blights of love have in them such a remainder of radiance that they make other happiness pale indeed. I came into the room at evening and he was sniffling. He did not want the lights on. He said it did not befit a man to cry. The electric ring was on and beside it a saucepan full of some brew. On the table, dripping, was a scarf. In fact the drips were what most caught my attention, and I worried about the carpet underneath.

'Believe me,' he said, 'it was beautiful, you will have to believe me.'

Then he put the light on and I saw what had happened. He had bought me a scarf, and having bought it in a second-hand shop, he had decided to wash it, but washing in his mind was confused with boiling, and the colours had run. What were once white and mauve stripes were now streaked with inter-shades of each and the bobbins at the bottom were as soft as squashed berries. I held it up and said that once it dried it would be the most beautiful thing, indeed not a scarf but a cape. Other gifts were nothing compared to it. I put it on the back of a chair with a bit of newspaper underneath and we listened for the drips. I expect it's in a police station now, or else burned, something like that.

One of those nights when he came back from the theatre and was sitting around, Wynne stood up on a chair, her hair plaited, the golden plait roped to one side, and for the edification of all sang 'Did you think I'd leave you out there when there's room on the horsey for two.' It was a very effective rendering, and of course contrived. It caused one of those impressive hushes so that people looked towards the ceiling or searched out the different shapes on the Persian carpet. I myself noticed that a dead fly had lodged inside the white light globe. It was a voice of pure unadulterated need. Had she been my daughter I would have jumped up, patted her instep, and the buckles of her patent shoes, said how sweet, how ingenuous, promised her a little bouquet, but she was not my daughter, she was my rival.

And I do believe it was she who got the wind up and got the law on to me. She probably smelt a rat. She probably wondered why I skedaddled so quickly, and did not appear at the inquest, why I could not be found. She saw us leave the theatre that fatal afternoon. Perhaps she followed us. I did think I heard a door bang, but made nothing of it, since doors banged unaccountably once the weather broke and no doubt doors are banging there still, and she is moping about in sack-cloth. Perhaps she loved him, perhaps it wasn't a mere schoolgirl crush. After the rendering he whispered if I would like a walk. We jumped up and borrowed the nearest coats off the hall stand. Walking down a steep cobbled street he had to hold me because my legs were running away with me. I was wearing very high heeled shoes. He said take them off. He carried them and we walked to a big gaunt stone square, one of the noblest left in the city. Most of the occupants were obviously preparing for bed as the lights shone chiefly from the upstairs windows. We walked about and joked about which house we would live in. We judged them mainly from the front gardens and the importance of the hall doors. He stood and selected one that had a beautiful stained-glass fan-light. Lights gleamed from behind it and the discs of various colours were like a rainbow sending arrows in several directions.

'Will you live with me?' he asked.

I could have fainted. There had been no hints about this, in fact the opposite. He and the others were threatening to go to a dance hall to find girls.

'Is it not precipitate?' I asked.

He said no. I made him happy. Nothing more or less. A score of questions might have occurred to me but the one that cropped up was what his parents and his close friends would say. He seemed to have anticipated it. His face in the moonlight was far from jovial, in fact his skin was strained from thought.

'We know how it is,' he said. I stood on his shoes so as to warm my feet. We held one another and I believe that I was holding on to a moment that I might preserve it for ever.

That night I decided to stay in my hotel. My mind was too agitated to be next to his. My mind hurried on to thoughts of a cottage, the university town where he was studying, a bicycle each, the days for our separate work, for errands, for shopping, for sawing wood, for clipping the hedges, for fetching the milk, the night for oil-lamps and a closeness as secure as a prayer. Purpose had been given back to me. It was only then as I was on the point of relinquishing it, that I saw how dreadfully I disliked the city, my routines and what passed for pleasure. I saw the hairdressers, the coveys of exasperated women perspiring under the drier; fashion magazines that paraded beautiful clothes one could not afford, and worse, beautiful accessories one could not afford! I thought of those dinners to which I went, and how politics used to be discussed, the cognoscenti talking, the onlookers, nodding sagely; or sex used to be discussed while someone advocated the case for plurality or versatility, and it always seemed as if we were all puppets, as if each of us had left our true selves in our wardrobes at home. It was easy to remember those occasions staring down at the entrée, at a piece of breaded veal, or cutting into the aspic around a salmon and wondering what one could possibly do to break through the shackles of politeness, and intrigue. I shall not miss these occasions, not one whit. No, nor the silly protocol after, as the women trooped to the bedroom to talk and sit and compete on thrones of upholstery. I brought Jude once and he proved to be as toadying as all the others. He made a point of telling some woman that she had the most beautiful breasts that he had ever seen. I expect he was admiring her collar of gold.

Of course I would go, I would be mad not to. Not to fill the common rut of days with some fleeting suggestion of happiness. I foresaw our winter as being cold and bracing, heavy falls of snow to keep us indoors, in our igloo, his body like a hound, mine softer and plumper, the firelight crackling, the flames making ring-a-rosy on our bare legs, on our bare haunches. How faithfully he would love me and how frequently. Like cat and mouse we would be waiting for the conquest of one another and the dreadful aftermath of tenderness. I had slept beside him for five nights and already I was missing the warmth, missing the sweet sly rascal approach, and all of a sudden the silly rhyme came to me about sugar and spice and all things nice. Everyone ought to have a halcyon time and I felt this was mine. It would not last, but that did not matter. Nothing would deter me, not doom, not death, not anointed ones, not caution, not conscience, not the tale of the suffering Christ. Oh what voluptuous hopes I fostered then.

When in the morning I went across I found him in the drawing room fully dressed. He looked a bit worried as if he feared a refusal. When I said yes he raised his arm and delivered a victory salute. I said who would be the one to tell my son, and I saw that he wanted to shirk it. I went upstairs and said to my son who was still sleeping, 'Come to the café with me.'

'What's up,' he said.

'Hart and I are thinking of living together.'

'Is that all,' he said and turned over and yawned. He was as happy, and as carefree as the best man at a wedding.

I took them all out to lunch. Our secret was conveyed from one to another and even Wynne found it incredible enough to be ridiculous. I received my first smile from her and saw that she had saddish eyes as if scales of white had been poured over cornflower blue so that the effect was of incipient blindness. They became so hearty that they went to their matinée tipsy and full of bravura. Out in the street they pretended to be a party of lunatics as they pulled faces at people and grimaced.

Alone in the house I wandered in and out of the various bedrooms. My instinct clamoured to clean the place up, to wash, scrub and fill the bureaux with jars of flowers. It was amazing, the quantities of combs, empty toothpaste tubes, ends of soap, buttons and used razor blades that had piled up. I made tea, and then sat in the drawing room so that I could look out the window, to the hills in the distance. Between me and them were the black spires, thickets of trees, the yellow and beige chimneys of the houses. I was trying to be reposed yet I was mindful of him. His return was what I really waited for, and the view of the hills merely hallowed the wait.

Then perhaps fear, or the lurking tip of it began to stir in me. It is only when there is sharp contrast that one can honestly admit what one feels about the preceding times. The empty rooms, the face-cream jars, the debris, these were one's life, while the lifting latch, his parted lips, kisses, a whirl in the air, these were one's dreams. Now they are both past life and dream, equally enhanced, equally distant by the mere fact of their being no more.

On the Wednesday Hart did not stay as usual to help with the tea and the slices of chocolate cake. He and I dashed off. We were walking down the street and he said, 'I want to draw your attention to this hole in the road.'

A huge mass of cobbles was arranged around the deep rectangular hole. We laughed at it and then we ran home to bed. I could run as fast but to flatter me he always lagged behind. I put a coloured shawl over the lampshade in the bedroom and we lay in a sphere of dappled light. It was raining outside. The pigeons cooed. He said three things were battling for his attention, the noise of the rain, a book about 'Hell's Angels' he had begun that morning and the love of me. Naturally I rebelled about being in third place but he said it was only to tease me, to vex me. He had a longing to see my anger in full flood. My son had told him that when my anger reached full spate the jugs and dishes shook on their hooks, along the dresser. He was eager for it as if this explosion was going to unite us. Perhaps he wanted to get it over with.

His fingers began to stray over my thighs, first the outside then the inside. Then he parted my thighs slowly and deftly. He was beginning to be more knowing and more daring. Then the diabolical happening. He quivered. Suddenly he was like a hooped fishing line, stiff and taut, and I could not get a word out of him.

'Jesus, he has gone mad,' I thought. The thing I dreaded most, in bed with a madman. Did I not see instantly my mad father with his long shins and his cuttlebone tongue stand over me, frothing. This erstwhile beautiful young boy began to tremor, began to froth, and then contort as if he was being wrung to death; a dreadful scream came out of his strangled chest, and the arteries on his temples had swelled up like rope. His tongue hung out, clueless, crazed. He was eating it. Blood spurted out of his mouth. Terrible obscene spasms as if his very desires had origined in the underworld. I screamed to him to stop it, stop it. A gyrating grotesque beast with a stone face stared at me as I kept telling it to stop it, and all the latent ugliness of the wide world was contained in it. Oh what metamorphosis. All the vileness of the world lavished on that thin frenzied body. Gone the boy with the long locks and a skin so white that when he blushed, it was if cochineal had been sprinkled over newly driven snow. Gone the smiling boy that even passers-by reached out to. I could never befriend that face again, that might at any moment convert itself into this other thing, this muck-sweat demon. Gone the Saint John of the Cross and instead the very features of a Lucifer but without intellect and without control. There was unleashed in me some great fund of hate and horror and I wonder now if hate had not been at the very seat of my love, or fear or disgust or lovelessness. Oh what mince it makes of my affections. Stripped of his beauty he was no more than a jack-in-the-box, something to be stuffed out of sight, disposed of at will. An object, a reject.

He tried desperately to say something, to mouth it, maybe to say get a pill, or get a doctor but it was in vain. He was writhing around, arching and twisting like a cobra, a fidget of a man. For the first time I felt the gruesome power of the hand that strikes. Love him – No. Be his companion – No. Grow old in his service – No. I had the breeches now, the upper hand. Gangsters, all would get their goriest comeuppance. It is true that I killed them, in killing him. Cruelly, lovelessly I would have ridden him until he snapped and broke except that his poor organ was limp and ragged. He begged for help, with the worst, the most humiliating, the most craven, the needful beg, and undoubtedly I saw my own begging famished self reflected in him and I took the pillow from under the bed cover, placed it across his contorted face, pressed with all my might, and held it there until he went quiet as a baby whose breath is almost inaudible. Except that his had snuffed out. I did not say my heart is in the coffin there with Hart, I did not say where my heart was. I think, due to its long awaited adventure my heart had burst apart and spread like entrails. Then very soon, which is to say seconds after, it was as if I had wakened and found my happiness to be unhappiness, hopes dashed or perhaps it was as if I had gone into a long sleep.

I got up. I half dressed. I removed every scrap of evidence. I lifted the pillow. It was then the eyes almost spoke and I knew I had already been introduced to that gaze in Florence when I saw the David, that stone gaze that speaks with an incomprehensible sorrow of man's passion, man's fear and man's murderousness. Because of course fear it was that had turned me into instant murderer. It seemed to me that even in death he seemed to manage a shaky smile and I thought – and oh how mad is a thought capable of being – that in fact I had done him a favour because now I was the one who would be damned and not he. All the dread I have ever dreaded began to take hold of me. It was like some terrible prophecy, on the verge of coming true. I had lost whatever it is in this world I had sought to gain – peace of mind maybe.

Yet I took the shawl off the lamp and switched off the light. You could say I managed to stagger out. Even as I did I already expected him to call, and the touching vision came to me of how one night when illicitly he came to my hotel bedroom, he put his clothes near the door, so that he could find them easily on the way out, so that he need not clamber about. I got out. I descended the stairs, leaning most carefully against the wall, realising that a bit of yellow wash would mark my black suede coat. In the street I rubbed it away. I was caution itself.

Two hours later I was on my way to the castle. While I was there nobody bothered me, that is apart from myself. I had the occasional bout of jitters but for the most part I flung myself into my work, indeed stared and stared at the old lady, smoothed and felt her good-natured cheek, felt her crabbed hands, talked to her, even asked her advice. I was going down to London, with my handbag full of samples, tiny specks of black, brown and bottle-green paint in folds of lint, taking them to be analysed.

IT WAS an evening flight. The clouds not far beneath gave the impression of being the backbones of millions of unshorn sheep all herded together in God's plentiful land. The sunset too was glorious, a long unbroken path of red skimming the skyline, and the sun's rim like the crown of a head just jutting, between cloud and burnished. Yet I felt restless. They served nothing, not even tea, and I kept opening my purse and looking in the little square tortoiseshell handmirror for signs. I even began to discuss with myself what the autumn would be like, and if things got too much, that is to say if it became dangerous, I could scoot. I hadn't dreamt of Hart in the ten nights since the event, not even once, and that was heartening. I tried not to think of the last thing he had said before he gasped. He said, 'The difficulty is, in convincing people that there is no difficulty.' Ah woe. Probably the very last word he said was no, or shit, or why, but that would have been inaudible and heard only by him. I asked the hostess for a pillow as I dearly wanted to nestle against it, to sleep, to forget. I also felt as if people were watching me and knew that that would be my future now, that hunted feeling.

As it came nearer to landing I looked out at the wing that was like a great serge bird dipping slowly in the sky. There was a little pencil of light at its far end, twinkling, and I called it Hope. Below a lake, a lagoon, water inching its way over brown mossy earth. I think I saw everything with the eyes of one who would not be seeing it again and that was my warning to me. Yet staring at the little pencil of light I asked God to let me free and I promised to atone till the day I died, in perpetual mourning if necessary. Even then I was hard put to it to admit that I had done wrong, because of not being able to face it, because of my full self, my sensible self being absent from the deed, from the involuntary deed. It was as if it had been done in sleep except that I was awake. I know I was awake because our eyes met and oh such a dumb speechless stare did I get, and it spoke multitudes.

'No smoking. Fasten belts' flicked on. I gathered myself into a clench and imagined myself as being a hedgehog preparing to land. We came down with the usual thud and clatter. Music was switched on and when I saw two policemen follow the movable stairs towards our plane I knew with certainty that my number was up.

'Nora, megirl, you're done for,' I said, and yet as they stepped on the plane, spoke to the hostess, and then strode towards me, I do believe that I mustered a smile.

I see the dawn or rather I feel the oncome of it. There is a chill. That kind of icy chill in the joints that only the warmth of another can take away. Another! The light has changed, not just the visible light, but something else – the mood that it imparts, the ghastly ghostly mood. But it will pass, like all else will pass, and morning with its perky youngness will no doubt come tripping in. And the terrors that rise up from below, that have not yet come to the surface, these too will have to be met.

Dawn, day, dark, frost, cloud, sprinkling, icicle, a fall of snow, bare places covered over, sparrows and red wings, daisy, hollyhock, wall marigolds ... Ah ye world that I hold dear, soon now you will be slipping away.